The crowd parted—and that's when he saw she was pregnant

Jeff calculated the months Bailey'd been gone. Seven. He looked over the size of her advanced pregnancy and realized it was his baby. He tried to sort out the rush of emotions, but they were too strong. The only one he could isolate was possession. His baby!

Jeff remembered the lovemaking they'd shared back in Bison City and found it hard to imagine that she could have been in love with anyone else when she was with him. Not Bailey.

Then she turned in his direction. For an instant he saw joy in her eyes, bright, clear, all for him. Then fear invaded. She closed her eyes quickly, but as though she couldn't help herself, she opened them and looked at him. All that was left in the brown depths was guilt.

Jeff knew without a doubt that the baby was his.

Dear Reader,

Welcome to another month of wonderful stories at Harlequin American Romance—where you'll find more of what you love to read. Every month we'll bring you a variety of plots from some of the genre's best-loved authors. Harlequin American Romance is all about the pursuit of love and family in the backyards, big cities and wide-open spaces of America!

This month you won't want to miss *A Cowboy's Woman*, the continuation of Cathy Gillen Thacker's series, THE McCABES OF TEXAS. This family of bachelors is in for some surprises when their parents take to matchmaking. And talented author Muriel Jensen brings us *Countdown to Baby*, the second book in the DELIVERY ROOM DADS series. In this three-author, three-book series you'll meet the McIntyre brothers of Bison City, Wyoming. They're in a race to see who'll have the New Year's first baby.

Also this month is Mollie Molay's *Daddy by Christmas*, a compelling story of blended families— just in time for the holidays. And Mindy Neff wraps up her TALL, DARK & IRRESISTIBLE duo with *The Playboy & the Mommy*.

Please drop us a note to tell us what you love about Harlequin American Romance and what you'd like to see in the future. Write to us c/o Harlequin Books, 300 East 42nd Street, 6th Floor, New York, NY 10017.

Happy reading!

Melissa Jeglinski
Associate Senior Editor

Countdown to Baby

MURIEL JENSEN

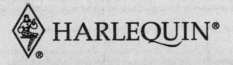

TORONTO • NEW YORK • LONDON
AMSTERDAM • PARIS • SYDNEY • HAMBURG
STOCKHOLM • ATHENS • TOKYO • MILAN • MADRID
PRAGUE • WARSAW • BUDAPEST • AUCKLAND

To all my readers—
my love and good wishes
as we embark on the new millennium.

ISBN 0-373-16798-9

COUNTDOWN TO BABY

Copyright © 1999 by Muriel Jensen.

This edition published by arrangement with Harlequin Books S.A.

® and TM are trademarks of the publisher. Trademarks indicated with
® are registered in the United States Patent and Trademark Office, the
Canadian Trade Marks Office and in other countries.

Visit us at www.romance.net

Printed in U.S.A.

ABOUT THE AUTHOR

Muriel Jensen and her husband, Ron, live in Astoria, Oregon, in an old Four-Square Victorian at the mouth of the Columbia River. They share their home with a golden retriever/golden labrador mix named Amber, and five cats who moved in with them without an invitation (Muriel insists that a plate of Friskies and a bowl of water are *not* an invitation!)

They also have three children and their families in their lives—a veritable crowd of the most interesting people. They also have irreplaceable friends, wonderful neighbors and "a life they know they don't deserve but love desperately anyway."

Books by Muriel Jensen

HARLEQUIN AMERICAN ROMANCE

Don't miss any of our special offers. Write to us at the following address for information on our newest releases.

Harlequin Reader Service
U.S.: 3010 Walden Ave., P.O. Box 1325, Buffalo, NY 14269
Canadian: P.O. Box 609, Fort Erie, Ont. L2A 5X3

Dear Reader,

When our editors asked us to write stories about three brothers who wind up in the delivery room near midnight, December 31, 1999, we sat down to think. Good-looking men, pregnant ladies with brains and beauty, and a first baby of the millennium contest—how could we resist?

The friendship we formed as we created DELIVERY ROOM DADS was an added bonus. E-mails flew fast and furious, and when the dust settled, we had a town, a family, a contest and happily-ever-after for everyone involved.

Welcome to Bison City, Wyoming, home of the devastating McIntyre brothers. The baby race begins in Karen Toller Whittenburg's *Baby by Midnight?* (October), complications arise in Muriel Jensen's *Countdown to Baby* (November), and the winner is revealed at the stroke of midnight in Judy Christenberry's *Baby 2000* (December). Our characters remind us of the love and strength of family. We hope they do the same for you, too. Thank you for joining us in the delivery room as these special dads ring in the new millennium!

Muriel Jensen
Judy Christenberry
Karen Toller Whittenburg

Prologue

April 1999

Jeff McIntyre rose slowly from sleep to wakefulness. His journey was accompanied by the remembered strains of some song about goodbye the band had played the night before, of the tactile memory of silken arms wrapped around his neck, of breasts squashed against his rib cage, of a plump bottom in his hands as life roared through him to the woman in his embrace, powerful and exquisite.

He came to full awareness with a start and opened his eyes, certain the past three days, and last night in particular, had been a figment of his imagination and he would find himself alone in his bed.

But Bailey was there, her warm, delicious weight sprawled over him, her long honey-blond hair covering his shoulder and snagged on the overnight beard on his jaw.

Happiness glowed inside him like a candle in a cave. This was it. *She* was it. The woman he'd come home to find. He didn't question the fact that he'd known her only three days. He was a McIntyre; a gift for decision was a legacy from his great-great-grandfather Samuel.

Jeff wrapped both arms tightly around Bailey, and even in sleep she reacted to his touch as she had all night long. She burrowed her face into his throat, flung a leg over him and strained to get even closer.

That single graze of her thigh brought him instantly to the edge of need. He tucked her leg up higher and swept his hand along the underside of it to the warm heart of her. She made a small, high sound he'd heard scores of times last night, and in a moment, eyes still closed, she rose over him and took him inside her.

Jeff erupted just as she tossed her head back, and the sun rose to flood the room with light. Usually, he wasn't one to think philosophically while making love, but he did this time. It was as though finding Bailey Dutton had opened every door life had so far held closed, and the future he'd begun to dream about opened itself to him.

This woman was meant for him.

BAILEY DUTTON came awake with a start as her body tightened then opened again like a frantic morning glory. The sense of fierce urgency that had become so wonderfully familiar during the long night now came upon her again, straining her to the brink of a whimper. Then she tossed her head back as everything in her body began to quake with a tumultuous and thorough fulfillment.

This man could not be real. After the long years of confinement caring for her mother, meeting Jeff

McIntyre had been like a shout of laughter at a wake, confusing but very welcome.

And to discover that he made love with the same elegant perfection with which he did everything else was almost more than she could bear. She'd had so little light in her life for so long that she felt blinded, disoriented.

Her body, however, suffered no such ambivalence. This was good, it thought, refusing to release him even after they'd drifted back to earth again. *I want this man. This is the man we thought we'd never have.*

''Yes,'' Bailey said, half-aloud, as her breathing and her body finally relaxed. He made her laugh, he made her sigh with longing, he brought her to the absolute pinnacle of lovemaking perfection and let her linger there as though the moment was infinite.

In a life that had been all about caring for her mother's life, then finally attending to her death, this concentration on herself was heady stuff. She wanted more. More.

While she still knelt astride him, his hand came up to smooth back the hair in her face. She put her hand to his and leaned into it, relishing his warm, possessive touch.

''I love you, Bailey,'' he said. ''I want you to stay.''

Sure. Of course, her body said. But her brain formed itself suddenly into a fist and punched her between the eyes. *Wake up! What are you thinking?*

Her eyes opened with the mental blow, and she stared in horror at the man lying against the pillows. Eyes the blue of a stormy sky watched her first in languid pleasure, then, as they saw her anxiety grow, in mounting concern. Every feature except those watchful eyes seemed to freeze—strong, straight nose, square jaw, frowning forehead.

She resisted the impulse to put a soothing hand to the wiry dark hair against the pillow. He'd never understand. She should have used her head instead of her heart.

She climbed off him, suddenly self-conscious about her nakedness, and pulled on the first thing she could find—his pleated white shirt from the wedding. It fell to midthigh on her and allowed her to say what she had to with some degree of modesty. Though it occurred to her that it was a little late for that.

"I could love you, too, but..." How could she possibly explain how much her new freedom meant to her? She stuttered and stammered, groping for words, but found none. She finally raised her arms in despair. "But I can't. I just can't." She gathered up the yards of garnet chiffon that was her bridesmaid's dress and slipped it on over her head.

When she emerged from it, she was face-to-face with a very angry man who hadn't bothered to put *anything* on.

"Pardon me?" he asked with a quiet politeness belied by the set of his jaw. "What do you mean, you could but you can't? Am I crazy, or doesn't that contradict itself?"

She walked around the room gathering up her strapless bra, panties, stockings, slip. She found the picture hat that matched her dress and draped the ribbons over her arm. "Jeff, I explained about my mother," she said breathlessly as she turned in a circle, trying to spot her shoes. He pulled a pair of jeans out of the closet and put them on. "I loved her dearly, but caring for her was a long, painful siege and I'm finally..." She knew the word she wanted to use was tied up with selfishness, but nothing else described what she needed in her life right now—not even love. "I'm free, Jeff. I haven't been free in five years."

She forgot about her shoes and went toward him, remembering in sharp detail every tender and passionate touch of his hands, every laugh he'd brought from deep inside her, every thought and feeling he'd shared that had made her feel connected and cared for.

"Please try to understand." She put a hand to his bare shoulder. "Josie's been talking to me or writing to me about her brothers for years. I felt as though I knew you. I related to you, particularly because you had to go to New York, too. But unconsciously Josie played a dirty trick on us when she paired us up for her wedding. You're everything any normal woman would want in her life, but everything I *don't* want right now."

He didn't move a muscle under her touch. "Freedom," he asked flatly, "is more important to you than love?"

Even as she accepted how out of tune that was with the world and the way it worked, she nodded. "For five years I sent designs to New York by fax because I had to be home in Portland with Mom. And while I don't resent a moment of that time, I'm now free to be where the action is. Someday I'm going to have my own design company, and the only way I can do that is to be there where it's all going on.''

JEFF WALKED PAST HER to his closet and yanked a cobalt-blue sweater off a shelf and pulled it on. When he emerged from it, he was face-to-face with a very distressed young woman. He was a little ashamed that he took a certain pleasure in her anguish.

Only a little ashamed.

And only a certain pleasure.

He walked past her to pull a pair of socks out of the top dresser drawer. ''The next time you sashay into a man's life,'' he said, sitting on the edge of the bed and pulling on his socks, ''you should wear a warning label behind your ear. 'Potentially harmful if made love to.'''

He bent to retrieve his shoe, spotted something red sticking out from under the bed and pulled it out. It was one of her shoes. He dug a little deeper and found the other. He tossed them to her one at a time.

She caught them, her cheeks pink with indignation. ''I didn't *sashay*. I came to rent a room. Considering you're the only hotel in town, and considering your sister recommended The Way Station as the place to stay, I didn't have much choice. The fact that our relationship went beyond that is your fault as much as mine.''

''I'm not denying responsibility,'' he said, pulling on and lacing his second shoe. ''I'm just saying I don't make a habit of sex for the hell of it, contrary to what a New York woman might think of a country boy.''

She rolled her eyes exasperatedly. ''Oh, please.

You spent eight years in New York—far longer than I have. It just got old for you so you came back to Wyoming, but you've still got that big-city gloss, so don't try to give me that country-boy story.'' Clutching her clothes, she gave him a final glare and started to walk away. ''And if that felt like sex-for-the-hell-of-it to you, then you need to have your head examined. And whatever else might benefit from a good—''

He caught her just as she reached the door, reminding himself that his instinctive reactions on how to deal with her smart mouth were now considered antiquated and sexist, and a jailable offense. And he'd only hate himself later. So he simply trapped her with her back to the door, a hand on it at either side of her head.

Fear flared in her eyes, then she angled her chin and stared him down. ''I spent all night in your arms,'' she said. ''You don't scare me. I know better.''

''My intention isn't to frighten you. I spent the night in *your* arms and I know better.'' He guessed that she was a little more upset than she was willing to reveal because she looked everywhere but at him. ''But if you've spent so much of your womanhood in isolation, you might bear in mind that dealing with a man is a little different from dealing with a boy. Feelings are involved as well as glands, and if you have no intention of sticking around, then don't act as though he's just hung the moon you made love under.''

Her eyes brimmed with tears suddenly, and she

wedged a space between their bodies. He let her push him back.

"I didn't *act* anything!" she said faintly but angrily. She turned to the door, stuck one hand out from her pile of things and struggled with the knob. She dropped a shoe and her panties.

He bent to get them for her, then opened the door. She snatched the shoe, thanked him stiffly and marched out into the hall toward the steps that curved down to the second floor. There was no elevator at The Way Station.

God. He didn't want it to end this way, even though it had only begun three days ago. He couldn't believe he was going to let her walk out of his life.

But this was a side of her he hadn't seen before. They'd been too taken with each other to talk about serious things, too fascinated with shared interests to get to the matters a man and a woman usually discussed when they had time on their side.

He tried to take part of her burden. "Let me help you down to your room."

She took a step back out of his reach, her eyes dark and unhappy. "No. There are people around. I'd like to maintain a little dignity and keep last night just between us."

He didn't have the heart to tell her there was little likelihood of that with a pile of underthings in her arms. She turned on her heel and started down the stairs.

He went to the railing to watch her descend, angry as hell that she could march off like that, her chin in the air, when she was taking with her everything he thought he'd finally found after a long, dry search.

He waited until she was on the gallery below.
"Bailey!" he called.
She leaned out to look up at him.
He dropped her silky panties on her upturned face.

Chapter One

Early November 1999

"Are you going to look Bailey up while you're in New York?" Josie asked.

The McIntyres sat around the living room after Sunday dinner. Matt, Jeff's older brother, sat in the big chair by the fireplace, their younger sister, Josie, and her husband, Justin, were close together on the love seat, and Jeff sat on the sofa. Alex, their younger brother, was in Texas on horse-training business.

Of course Justin wasn't a McIntyre, but even though he'd been married to Josie only seven months, he seemed like one.

The room still remained pretty much the way their parents had left it when they retired to Florida eight years ago and left the ranch in Matt's capable hands.

Jeff smiled, carefully withholding any other reaction to the question. None of his family knew what had happened that fateful wedding weekend, and he liked it that way. They tended to be meddlesome where each other's private lives were concerned, so he pretended not to have one.

"No, there won't be much time," he said. "I'm just going to sign the papers for the sale of that place I shared with Paul and Marty in the Hamptons. And I had a few things there I'm going to ship back. I'll just be a couple of days."

Josie was clearly disappointed. "I thought you two got along well while she was here."

"We did. She was fun. But I'm going with a purpose, and what little time I have for partying will be spent with the guys at the agency."

Jeff hadn't heard a word from Bailey in seven months and had accepted, with a sense of having made a lucky escape, that what they'd had was over before it had really begun.

He was no longer angry, just indifferent. Bailey Dutton didn't matter to him anymore. He picked up the sports section of the Sunday paper, spread it out on the coffee table and went for the football stats.

"I was hoping if you saw her," Josie persisted, "that you could get a catalog of the design firm's children's clothes." She patted her mounded stomach. "We're going to be needing them pretty soon."

Justin rolled his eyes at her brothers and put an arm around her shoulder. "Josie, you can get her to send you a catalog. If Jeff doesn't want to see her, he doesn't want to see her."

She folded her arms over her stomach. "Well, it's a small thing to ask. He'll be right there. The company she works for is just a couple of blocks away from his old agency." She narrowed her gaze on him. "I think something happened between them that he hasn't told us."

"Then it shouldn't come up for discussion," Jus-

tin said reasonably, "should it? Just because I bit the
dust over you, it doesn't mean Jeff shouldn't remain
a free man. What do you think, Matt?"

Matt gave him a warning look over his shoulder
as he added a log to the fireplace. "I'm happy on
my own, thank you very much. But I like the idea
of persecuting Jeff until he comes home with a bride.
What do you say, Jeff?"

"Nice guy, Matt. Hang me out to dry, why don't
you?" Jeff looked up from the paper. "And the
Chiefs lost to the Cowboys. You owe me five
bucks."

Matt frowned at him over his shoulder as he
wielded the poker at the burning tinder. "You're kidding. Dallas lost their linebacker for the rest of the
season."

"I know, but the rookie's good. I told you, but
you wouldn't listen to me."

"Could we get back to the issue of women!" Josie
said loudly.

"Of course." Jeff returned his attention to the paper. "Always happy to talk about them. Just don't
want to have to live with one."

"Amen," Matt said. The new log caught, Matt got
to his feet, dusted his hands off on the legs of his
jeans and resumed his chair.

"You're just afraid you won't find anyone like
Julie again." Josie spoke with little-sister candor.

"Jocasta!" Justin frowned at her. "That's enough.
And none of your business."

Josie's brothers laughed. He looked up at them in
surprise.

"There isn't a topic in this family that's none of

her business," Matt explained. "But don't let us stop you. Go ahead and try to keep her quiet. That'll be entertaining for all of us."

Jeff looked at her over the edge of his paper. "We've been trying to do that since she was born and completely ruined our bastion of male superiority. We had Mom wrapped around our fingers until she came into the picture."

Matt propped his booted feet on the stone hearth bench. "You wouldn't have believed the fuss just because we took her for a ride on old Rusty when she was eight months old. She liked it, but when Mom found us, the little traitor started to cry and carry on. Mom was convinced we were trying to kill her."

"I remember that," Jeff said with a scolding look at Josie. "You got us all tanned and grounded. That horse was so old, we could walk faster than he ran."

"Don't blame me. It was Matt's idea, Mathew." She fixed him with a serious look. "You have to get on with your life. And you." She turned to Jeff. "You could do this little thing for me. You could—"

Justin raised the hand resting lightly on Josie's shoulder and moved it to cover her mouth. "Sometimes when dealing with her," he said, "you have to have an alternative to reason."

She pulled his hand down. "But I could still use a catalog." Then she raised her own hands to stop everyone's objections. "Not for reasons of romance, but because all the pregnant women in this town could really do something for a designer of children's clothes."

Justin focused on her in pretended concern. "You

are aware that you're going to give birth to a *baby,* not a toddler. Babies don't wear anything but blankets.''

''What?'' Willie walked into the room with a tray of coffee. She was Matt's housekeeper, and had been with the McIntyres since Alex was in diapers. ''Where have you been? Babies wear layette gowns, sleepers, rompers. For a man about to have one, you don't know very much, do you?''

They'd all long-ago accepted that Willie's outspokenness was part of her charm.

Justin laughed. ''Josie's put me in the poorhouse buying books on the subject. She knows everything, so all I have to do is spoil him and hold him.''

Willie poured coffee into cups and handed them around. ''Honestly. In my day you had to wait for the baby to be born to know what it was going to be. Nowadays you just look inside a woman with a machine and know if you're having a boy or a girl. Takes all the mystery out of it.''

''Helps you to know what to expect,'' Justin reasoned. ''I might have been learning to sit through the ballet, when now I know I should be loosening my pitching arm.''

Willie scoffed at that with a wave of the napkin she handed him. ''Just expect your life to be turned upside down, whatever the baby is. Looking through a woman with a machine!'' she said again in wonder. ''The world's gone mad.''

Justin leaned forward to reach for the cream. ''If only there was a machine to tell you what she was thinking. *That* would be progress.''

Jeff shook his head. "It would only further confuse us. It's better this way."

Josie took Justin's chin in her hand and kissed him. "Poor things," she said with a shake of her head. "You don't understand us, because you're the ones who don't make sense."

"No." Justin took her hand and pulled it gently down. "I operate on reason. You operate on emotion. That's why I have trouble understanding you."

"In family matters," she argued amiably, "reason doesn't apply. Emotion does."

"How can reason ever not apply?"

"Because life does the unexpected every time you turn around. You can respond to that with laughter or tears, but not reason, because it doesn't make sense."

Justin considered that for a moment, then turned to each of Josie's brothers in complete bewilderment.

They laughed in unison. Matt smiled wryly. "Welcome to the family."

Josie struggled to reach for something under the paper, but the obstruction of her pregnancy made it difficult. She pointed instead. "Honey, could you get that folder, please? Thanks."

Justin produced a manila folder with a copy of their sonogram glued to the front of it. Josie put it on what was left of her lap and pulled out a sheet of paper, which she handed to Jeff.

"Call me illogical if you want to," she said, "but the hospital board is happy with me. My contest is making money for the new pediatrics wing."

Matt put his cup down. "I know. I've been hearing

about it in town. But the hospital's only three rooms. How can they add a pediatrics *wing?*''

"The wing's only one room, maybe two if the budget stretches that far. But with it, we'll be able to keep children overnight right there instead of sending them to Sheridan. The hospital has a donor for the wing, but asked the Bison City Women's League to help fund the extras. Toys, books, games—whatever we can provide.''

Jeff tried to make sense of the names and dates that appeared on the sheet. The only pattern he could find was that the dates were all the end of December and early January. And all the names were women's.

"There are fourteen women in this town," Josie said, "who are expecting babies around the end of the year."

Jeff nodded. "That would mean they were conceived when? March or April? The hiatus between the end of football season and the beginning of baseball. Gotta have something to do if you're not into basketball or hockey."

She drew a breath patiently. "My point is that we've gotten the ball rolling with the contest—a dollar to guess the time of birth of the first baby of the year. The merchants who usually give gifts to the first baby of the year are giving huge amounts of really special stuff to mark the millennium. So I figured if we get every pregnant woman in the county to enroll herself and her baby for five dollars, we could make enough to supply lots of toys." She patted Justin's hand. "And Mr. Mayor, here, thinks it'll be good for Bison City. Get us a little attention in the news and by word of mouth. That never hurts, especially if you're trying to attract tourists and business."

Jeff tried to figure out why she would want him involved and failed. "You want me to get somebody pregnant?" he teased.

She put both hands over her face, then dragged them down to her lap. "No, Einstein, we need someone who knows the ins and outs of advertising to help us get county-wide attention. I know you left the business because you didn't like it anymore, but all you have to do is help us figure out an approach, write a little copy and send us on our way. We'll take it from there."

Jeff thought through the few details she'd told him. "I don't see how you're going to make that much money. I mean, out of all the women who are pregnant in the county, how many would be due at the end of December? Even with the odds on your side, you'd make a couple of hundred dollars tops. The part about giving a dollar to guess the time of birth is good, but there again your profits are limited."

She nodded. "But for our little hospital, that's a lot of money. And we can do a lot with it."

"When's this all going to happen?"

"The church holds the Thanksgiving Fair the third weekend in November and we always draw people from all over the county. We'll advertise in the paper before that, then have a big booth at the fair and get everybody signed up. What do you think? Can you help us?"

"Sure." He handed Josie the sheet. He'd been supporting her schemes since she'd been seven and opened a lemonade stand with a friend on the sparsely traveled road on the ranch's northern boundary. He and Alex had posted a detour sign on the main road while Matt coerced his friends to stop by the stand.

Again they'd gotten in trouble. The highway department had taken exception to Jeff's creative approach to marketing, and Matt had apparently used a form of blackmail his friends' parents had objected to.

But Josie had made enough money to buy something for their mother for her birthday, and Jeff and his brothers had felt vindicated.

It was an attitude that survived to this day. It was strange, he often thought, that he'd gone to New York after college because his family had been so close and so strong that he'd doubted his abilities as an individual. He'd wondered if he could function and survive without them.

His gift for understanding people had made him very good at advertising. He could pick out precisely what it was about a product that would appeal to a target audience and make that product look as though it would round out their lives.

Then one day at a party he heard himself talking to his friends as though he had something to sell, instead of simple friendship to offer, and he decided he'd had enough. He was tired of spins instead of truths.

And he longed suddenly for the simplicity of home. Not that the people were simple, but the relationships were. You didn't have to sell anyone anything—they were with you because they were family, or neighbors.

He'd learned that he could live without his family, but he no longer wanted to.

He'd explained that to the account executive he'd been living with for several months, and she'd looked at him as though he was crazy. And made it clear that if he moved back to Wyoming, he was going alone.

So he did.

Josie threw her arms around him. "I'll try to get some solid ideas together while you're in New York, then maybe we can get serious about it when you get back?"

"If you're running this, Josie," Matt asked, "are you eligible to be entered in the contest?"

She nodded. "Justin thought of that. As long as all the funds and entries are held and handled by a neutral party, it's okay. Gunderson and Grebe, CPAs are doing it for us as their contribution to the whole thing."

He smiled at his sister. "Now, see? If Justin's logical mind hadn't pointed that out to you, your emotional approach to the whole thing might have made you ineligible to win."

"Well, of course," she agreed. "That's why we take on husbands."

"Take on?" the three men questioned in concert.

"Put up with," she rephrased. "For a good balance. Otherwise we could run the world ourselves."

There was a moment's silence, then Justin tickled her in retribution until she apologized. The two dissolved into laughter.

Jeff looked across the room at Matt, who shook his head over their antics, his eyes reflecting what Jeff felt—part relief that he didn't have to put up with such a level of emotion every day, and part jealousy that Justin had learned to cope with it.

Chapter Two

New York still engendered the excitement in Jeff that it had ten years ago. The difference was that now he understood excitement didn't mean fulfillment.

He called his friends from his hotel room, met to seal the sale of the house in the Hamptons, and went out to pack up and ship the things he'd left there.

Then on his last day in New York, he went to the agency to reconnect with a few colleagues he hadn't seen yet. That took him by the photo studio on the tenth floor where the sound of children's voices made him pause and look in.

He did a rapid double take.

No, he wasn't seeing things. Bailey Dutton stood there, surrounded by children who listened attentively while she spoke. A photographer and an older woman waited patiently near a set that looked like a school bus stop.

Jeff, in shock, made an instant discovery that was painful to accept. He wasn't over her at all. Everything he'd felt and thought during that long night of making love to her surfaced in him as though it had been held under pressure all this time and her presence had blown the lid off it.

Even as he wondered what she was doing here, he felt the deep-down truth that she was his. He knew that with every heartbeat and every breath.

The tough thing to accept, he thought reluctantly, was that probably he wasn't hers. She'd said she preferred freedom to love and had meant it. She appeared to have coped just fine without him. The children giggled at something she said, and she laughed with them, then wrapped her arms around them in a communal hug.

On closer inspection he noticed that she'd cut her hair, an act tantamount to a crime, if anyone was interested in his opinion. The honey-blond bob that curled behind her ears and had that fashionably mussed look was very smart, but it broke his heart. His thoughts of making love were now forever linked to the sweep of silky hair across his abdomen, his thighs, that part of him that would always remember her.

And her face looked a little thinner, though it still had that all-American-girl glow that had drawn him instantly to her.

He should nobly walk in and say hello, ask her how she was, pretend he was fine with the way things had turned out.

But he didn't have the guts to get that close. It hurt even from here to see her, to remember. He didn't want to look right into her eyes and see she was fine without him.

He turned to slip away at the same moment the

children left her and took their places on the set. And he saw her bulbous belly under a green wool dress.

First, he felt as though the world had stopped, as though a cosmic silence had fallen. Then he felt as though someone had taken that moment to punch him in the face. *That baby should have been mine!* a voice roared jealously inside him. *I was the one who— Wait a minute!*

He tried to clear his mind of the initial shock of her condition and calculate the months of her absence. Seven.

He looked at the size of her considerably advanced pregnancy and realized that unless she'd made love with someone around the time she'd made love with him…that *was* his baby.

He put a hand to the doorway as emotions rushed through him. He tried to sort them out, but they were too strong, too inextricably connected. The only one he could isolate for certain was possession.

His baby!

He took two steps into the room, then stopped himself, reason still at work despite the overpowering emotions. She could have made love with someone right after she'd left him. She could have had someone else in New York all the time. After all, she'd only spent three days in Bison City.

He remembered their lovemaking and found it hard to imagine that her heart could have been connected to anyone else, but she had a self-proclaimed need for freedom. Maybe that meant she could somehow disconnect heart from body in times of—

Suddenly aware of his presence, she turned in his direction. For an instant he saw joy in her eyes, bright, clear, all for him. Then turbulence took over and fear invaded. She looked away quickly and closed her eyes, but, as though she couldn't help herself, she opened them again and looked up at him.

All that was left in the soft brown depths was guilt.

He knew without a doubt that the baby was his.

Possession swelled in him again without restraint, and in the clarity of the moment all the other complicated things he was feeling identified themselves—anger, betrayal, revenge. And somewhere deep inside, though he fought it valiantly, was a reluctant tenderness toward her awkward yet beautiful body and the weary look in her eyes.

He put that last emotion aside as he strode into the room.

Bailey met him in the middle, clearly aware of what he was thinking, and caught his arm, trying to pull him toward the door. He resisted.

"Please," she said quietly. "The room is full of children." She freed his arm and walked out into the hallway.

He followed, pulling the studio door closed behind him.

BAILEY STOOD UNCERTAINLY in the middle of the hallway, heart pounding, the damnable nausea rising in her throat. He was here! Here! God *was* out to get her. She'd suspected it six months ago when she'd learned that one night with Jeff McIntyre—even though she'd left him—had effectively destroyed the freedom she'd waited for so long.

Jeff marched after her and stopped with just inches between them. Offices opened onto the hallway and employees and clients hurried by, some calling greetings to Jeff. He ignored them.

"Explain to me," he demanded softly but angrily, "why you're having my baby and didn't bother to tell me!"

"What are you *doing* here?" she asked, unable to resist the question in spite of all the other important details clamoring for answers.

He shifted his weight impatiently. "I came to sell a house I owned with a couple of friends. What in the hell are *you* doing here?"

"The design company I work for hired the agency and I came to…supervise the shoot. Look." She drew a deep breath to fight the nausea. In the pressure of the morning's shoot, she'd forgotten her Phenergan. "Let's go to my place. I'll expl—"

"We're staying right here," he insisted "Start talking."

"Jeff…" Nausea rose in her throat. She drew another breath and forced it back. "I'm just a couple of blocks from here. We'll be there in five— Oh, no!"

She put both hands to her mouth as her insides roiled again with new power. Her eyes must have registered her desperation.

Jeff caught her arm, pulled her several feet down the hall into an employees' lounge. He opened another door inside and pushed her in. She was thrilled to see white porcelain.

She emerged several moments later feeling empty—physically, spiritually, emotionally. But the mound of her stomach was reassuring proof to the contrary. She patted it comfortingly as she walked out into the lounge.

Jeff waited for her, arms folded, brow furrowed. She couldn't tell if he was angry or concerned. But, considering what he'd just discovered, she could guess.

"I thought nausea came with the beginning of a pregnancy," he said.

She nodded. "It does. I just have an overabundance of HCG." His frown deepened in question and she explained with a breath, "It's a hormone that makes you nauseous. I've managed pretty well, but every once in a while the wrong food or...or upset will set me off."

"Your face is thinner."

"I'm happy for that." She tried a smile. "Those chipmunk cheeks in a grown woman aren't very flattering."

The smile bounced right off him. He was like a stone mock-up of a gorgeous man propped in the middle of the lounge. Except that stone never looked as volatile as he did.

"You have a coat?" he asked.

She pointed back toward the studio. "I left it..."

"Get it. We'll go to your place."

She wasn't accustomed to letting anyone push her around, but she had to concede that she was at fault here, and he had to be allowed some latitude for shock.

She lived on the third floor of the Hudson Hotel Apartments in a small but adequate three rooms that she'd decorated on a tight budget but with a lot of verve. Or so she'd thought.

She put on the kettle to make tea as Jeff wandered around, hands in his pockets, his reaction indeterminate to her Lautrec posters, and the French country atmosphere she'd tried to create.

His tall, broad-shouldered presence in the small rooms seemed out of place, though he wandered around as though perfectly comfortable. Angry, but comfortable.

She walked out of the kitchen with a full teapot and two mugs, determined to answer all his questions and take control of the encounter. She deposited them on a square oak table she'd squeezed in by the window, between her plump sofa and the escritoire.

He pulled her chair out, a gesture that surprised her considering his anger. She sat.

He looked out on the canyon of tall buildings, then at the confined space inside and asked in apparent confusion, "This is freedom?"

She was determined to be patient. "Freedom is inside you," she said. "I feel free here."

She made a production of pouring tea so that he wouldn't see that that had become a lie. She had felt very free here until about a month ago. Then she began to realize how alone she was at a time when she was about to do something monumental—something that should be done with a husband and mother fussing around, with sisters standing by to help.

But she had none of those.

Fear, she'd discovered, seriously impinged upon freedom.

He sat down, ignoring his tea. "You were about to explain," he prodded, "why you chose not to tell me we're having a baby."

All right. It was time to take control. She fixed him with what she hoped was a firm look. But he had one of his own going on at the moment that put hers to shame. Still, she gave it her best.

"First of all, *we're* not having a baby, *I* am." Her voice came out steady and clear. She took courage from that and went on. "I was going to tell you next month. At first I was so sick I was afraid I might lose it, and then when I was sure she was going to be all right…" She had to be honest; she wished she had an alternative, but there was none. "I remembered how you are. You like things your way and preferably right now. Well, I didn't want to have to deal with that when I was sick a lot and work was really busy."

He'd stiffened the moment she began to speak, but he hadn't tried to interrupt or even to challenge anything she said. She took that as a good sign.

It would occur to her later that she should have known better.

"I apologize for that." Success was making her magnanimous. "I should have told you right away. But you can relax about it. I don't want child support, and I don't hold you responsible in any way."

She expected his features to relax after she'd absolved him of whatever duties he might have feared. But the opposite happened. His angry eyes grew darker as he pushed the teapot side and leaned toward her.

"This is the way it's going to be," he said in a tone just as steady and clear as hers had been but with an edge of authority she found impressive even while she bristled under it. "I'm flying out of here tonight, and you're coming with me."

She opened her mouth to insist that she was not, but he raised a hand for silence. She was so astonished by his arrogance that she complied.

"You're going to stay with me through the birth of the baby," he went on as though he was reading an edict at court. "After that, we'll decide what to do."

She tried several times to speak, but was so incensed, she finally demanded in a choked voice, "Who do you think you are?"

"The father of your baby," he replied. "Finish your tea, then start packing. I'll call the airport."

She slapped her napkin on the table and pushed herself to her feet. It wasn't easy—or pretty—but she did it. "You cannot take over my life like that!" she shouted at him. "This baby is mine, too, and I finally have the career I've wanted most of my life, and you're not going to take it from me!"

"I don't want to take it from you," he replied calmly. "I don't want a woman to whom freedom is more important than love. But I want my baby. So you'll stay with me until she's safely delivered, then we'll draw up custody terms."

His features softened suddenly and he asked with artless emphasis, "She? You know it's a girl?"

She nodded. "I asked to be told when I had an ultrasound."

She tried not to be distracted by the suggestion of a smile on his lips. She had a score of arguments against his plan and, on the other hand, at least a score of things that had definite appeal. The foremost of which was that it gave her a valid excuse to be with him.

But she might grow to really like being with him, and everything she'd planned for herself—the vast, unfettered life she'd dreamed about—would disappear.

"No," she said. "I'm not going with you."

He took her arm and pushed her gently back down into her chair. "Let me put it to you another way." He spoke with a calm dispassion she didn't like at all. "You do this for me, or when the baby's born, I'll sue you for full custody."

Nausea roiled in her stomach. She looked into his eyes, trying to assess how serious a threat that was, and was horrified to see that it was genuine.

"You wouldn't!" She tried to delude herself.

"Did I tell you," he asked, leaning back in his chair, "about Great-great-grandfather Samuel McIntyre?"

She was beginning to understand the wily workings of his mind well enough to know this could not be the non sequitur it sounded like. She waited for him to go on.

"He came to San Francisco from Boston around the Horn on the *Lucky Wind* in 1872 with two saddlebags of gold with which to start a bank in the West. He was twenty-six. On the ship, he met Jocasta Kearney, a young woman from Philadelphia who was on her way to join her father."

Bailey failed to see how the story related, but was interested despite herself.

"A storm not far from their destination wrecked the ship, and the passengers were forced overboard.

Samuel jumped with his saddlebags of gold and Jocasta. But Jocasta wasn't a good swimmer and the water was rough. Sam couldn't save her and the gold, so he dropped the bags and took Jocasta to safety.''

Bailey didn't quite get the parallel. ''Josie's given name is Jocasta,'' she said, trying to think it through. ''So I presume Jocasta Kearney became your great-great-grandmother.''

''That's right.''

''But how does that relate to your threat to seek custody of Noelle?''

''Of...who?''

She firmed her jaw, prepared to defend her choice of names for the baby. ''Noelle. She's due around Christmas. I like it. We were talking about the parallel.''

''Right.'' He pushed her teacup toward her. ''Samuel had decided that Jocasta was his. Love and family have always been more important to a McIntyre than gold or anything else. Even freedom.''

Bailey felt a small ripple of excitement along her spine. She couldn't help it. Freedom had been everything to her for a long time, until Jeff McIntyre had confused everything for her.

Now she sometimes found herself wondering if this was freedom. And not just because of the baby. She understood the baby would compromise her freedom somewhat, but she thought that would be fine, because the baby would be hers.

There were other things she'd expected freedom to bring with it that seemed to be missing, and she couldn't analyze what they were. Of course, she was

in her third trimester, she thought with a sigh. Sometimes she was lucky to remember her name.

She met his eyes, trying to analyze what he'd
meant by that analogy. A moment ago he'd said he
wouldn't want a woman who valued freedom over
love. But he'd just said, "Samuel had decided that
Jocasta was his." That little thrill played along her
spine again. She hated that it did; she didn't want it
to. She didn't want to belong to anyone for a long,
long time.

But even in the midst of the career successes of
the past six months, memories of him would come
back to her in quiet moments, and she would remember the safety she felt in his company, the security
he'd inspired in her because he was so sure of who
he was.

He straightened her out on that score with cool
brutality. "Relax," he said. "After what you've
pulled, you could never be my family. But the baby's
mine, and I'll do whatever it takes to get her."

Bailey ran to the bathroom to be sick.

When she'd finished, Jeff helped her to her feet
and put a cold wet washcloth to her face.

"No wonder you've gotten scrawny," he said,
folding it over and reapplying it. "I can't believe
you're this ill and you're just supposed to live with
it."

"I have pills," she said as he dried her face with
a towel. "I forgot…to take them this morning. I had
to meet the children early."

"Where are the pills?"

She opened the medicine cabinet and pulled out

the small brown bottle. He filled a paper cup with water.

She looked at her options while she downed a pill, then a second cup of water. If she let Jeff take her to court, she wasn't sure how her simple little life would fare against Jeff's share of the McIntyres' small but powerful empire and his successful hotel business. It was entirely possible she could lose Noelle to him.

On the other hand, if she went with him, she had a terrible fear he'd have difficulty letting her leave with the baby even if they were able to compromise on shared custody. The possessiveness he'd displayed so far didn't bode well for it at all.

JEFF WATCHED HER mull over the decision as she swallowed the pill.

He was still furious with her, felt betrayed that she could have shared his bed and then done this to him, but everything else he'd felt for her during those three days still lived inside him like grass pushing up through the sidewalk. His feelings shouldn't be there, but they were. And they were making things happen.

He had to get her home with him. He had to see if there was any way they could pull their lives together. And, barring that, he had to see his baby safely born and make certain, legally if he had to, that he would have a place in her life.

"Why'd you cut your hair?" he asked as she replaced the pills and put the cup in the trash basket.

She smiled wryly. He caught a glimpse of the woman from the wedding weekend. "Because it was always in the way when I was sick. This is much easier.''

He still felt mournful about her long, golden waves. ''You had the most beautiful hair I'd ever seen.''

She looked at him a moment, connecting, he guessed, with the same thing he was remembering. ''Yeah, well, I'm not a bridesmaid anymore. That was like a weekend out of time. Stolen.''

''Is that why you're trying to give it back?''

Her shoulders sagged wearily and she walked out of the bathroom. He followed her to a small yellow bedroom in which there was barely space to move between the double bed and the dresser. He stayed in the doorway.

''That's something I didn't miss about you,'' she said, folding up a decorative screen that stood in front of a doorless closet. She leaned it in the corner.

''What's that?''

''The complex arguments. You've always got an answer for everything.''

''Most things *do* have an answer.''

''Not when you really consider both sides.''

''Why should I do that?'' he asked. ''I just consider the side that works for me.''

She turned in indignation, clothes draped over her arm, then apparently saw something in his face that told her he was kidding.

''I don't miss that, either,'' she said with a scolding look at him as she tossed her things onto the bed. ''You love to put me on.''

He was careful not to betray triumph. She was packing! ''No, I like to watch you get indignant. I think the pink cheeks and the fluster are more you than the cool career woman. Can I use the phone in the kitchen?''

''Sure.''

He started to walk away, but she called his name with a note of desperation that brought him right back. She stood in the doorway, her eyes concerned but her mouth determined.

''You have to promise me that if I come with you in good faith, you won't try to take Noelle away from me.''

''Are you going to promise me that you won't fight me on shared custody?''

''What do you mean by shared?''

He'd been thinking about it. ''I know fifty-fifty isn't reasonable, but summers, some holidays.''

She stared at him as though surprised. Then she said, the line of her mouth softening, ''That could work.''

He had the most overwhelming urge to kiss that mouth, but he knew when not to press his advantage. ''Then, I won't take you to court. We'll just have a lawyer draw something up.''

''Okay.''

''Good.''

Jeff called the airport and arranged for a second ticket. Then he turned the phone over to Bailey, who called her boss.

He warmed a can of soup and pretended not to listen as she explained in lengthy but nebulous terms about being tired, needing a break during this last part of her pregnancy and having an opportunity to visit a friend.

She was stopped midsentence, then said with a sigh, "Yes. Uh-huh. Yes. Well, I didn't know he was coming. No. He didn't know I was here, either." She listened for a few moments, then cast him a glance he pretended not to see. "Yes, he is. And there are two more at home just like him. Isn't that a scary thought? Yes of course I'll be back."

Dutifully stirring soup, he didn't even look her way. She was not coming back if he could help it.

And if he couldn't... McIntyres were taught not to think in terms of negatives. Another legacy from Samuel.

He was going to spend the next two months convincing Bailey that love was more important than freedom. She was going to love his family, love the hotel, love Wyoming, and by January she was going to love him.

And so would Noelle.

Chapter Three

Jeff and Bailey caught the red-eye out of Kennedy to Chicago, then flew on to Casper in a night that was two hours longer than usual because they'd traveled west.

Bailey, exhausted, didn't seem to mind. When her head lolled sleepily against the back of her seat, he pushed up the armrest between them and settled her against him. The flight attendant brought him a blanket, and they crossed three states while Bailey slept.

That was when he experienced one of his life's most amazing moments. His daughter kicked him in the gut.

Bailey was cradled against him, her bulbous belly pressed against his abdomen. For an instant, he wasn't sure what had happened, and then he felt it again and realized what it was—a small but very sure kick.

He found it amazing. More amazing even than the fact that tons of metal filled with people could travel through air. That was only physics. This was life!

BAILEY WOKE somewhere over Nebraska, her cheeks flushed from sleep, her hair mussed. She pushed against him, blinking, and looked around her. Then she straightened away from him even farther when she realized she'd been leaning against him. "How long have I been sleeping?" she asked, her voice raspy.

He smoothed a lock of her hair that was sticking up. "In real time or considering the time zones?"

She punched his shoulder halfheartedly. "You're doing it again."

"Sorry." He looked at his watch. "About three hours. You getting hungry?"

She sighed and peered out the window at the thin line of dawn in the deep banks of blue. "I'm always hungry. But I'd better not eat anything until we're off the plane, just in case."

"That won't be for another hour."

BAILEY YAWNED and leaned back in her seat, newly convinced about just how difficult these two months were going to be. All she'd had to do was doze off, let her vigilance slip for one instant, and she'd been right back in his arms. This was not good. Not good at all.

She adjusted her seat belt and smoothed her hair with her fingers. The plane was still dark, and she was trying to neutralize its shadowy intimacy by pretending it didn't exist.

"You didn't tell Josie about us," she said. This was a matter they were going to have to deal with sooner or later, and the best way to do that was straight on. It took the romance out of the situation—

and whatever potential it had to draw her into its snare.

"It's a pact Matt and Alex and I have." He closed his eyes, diluting the effects of her efforts. She sat up a little straighter. "We try never to tell her anything, so she won't either worry or try to manage the problem for us, whatever it is. Anyway, there was nothing to tell—or so I thought."

Bailey sighed, imagining her friend's reaction to her pregnancy. They'd corresponded several times since the wedding, and Bailey hadn't mentioned how she and Jeff had felt about each other, or that she was pregnant.

"She's going to be mad at us," Bailey predicted.

Jeff shook his head and closed his eyes. "No, she's going to be mad at *you*. I couldn't tell her what I didn't know."

All right. She wouldn't think about that now. The moment would be upon her soon enough.

"How're Matt and Alex?" she asked. Though she hadn't gotten really well acquainted with his brothers, she liked them. Not only did they all look very much alike, but Matt and Alex seemed to be opposite ends of the Jeff scale—Matt being older and more serious, Alex younger and a little wild. They all shared the McIntyre wit and charm.

"Matt's fine," he said, eyes still closed. But she saw a pleat form on his brow. "At least, as fine as he's going to be for a while."

Bailey knew that some years ago Matt had lost his wife, Julie, who'd been five months pregnant with their son, in an automobile accident.

"Then I guess it's a blessing that of all of you,

he's the one who loves to run the ranch. There must be enough details there to keep five minds occupied."

"True. But he's a family man at heart. Work alone will never make him happy." He was quiet for a moment, then he added as though it were an afterthought instead of blatant campaigning, "Just like freedom won't do it for you."

"Jeff..." she warned.

"You asked. I supposed Josie told you Alex is training horses in Texas. Eventually he wants to set up a breeding program at the ranch. Matt and I think he's nuts, but then we always have."

Bailey smiled about that. "Yes, Josie wrote me about him. But what about... What was her name? Annie? I thought they were serious."

"Annie Thatcher. They've been on and off since grade school. She's been more patient than any man deserves—particularly Alex. She's expecting, too, about the same time as Josie." He opened his eyes suddenly and turned his head toward her. "And the same time as you."

"You mean...Alex's baby?"

"There's been no outright announcement, but we all think so. We're just being quiet about it until she says something. Or Alex does."

She rolled her eyes. "More McIntyres for the new millennium. That would be a frightening thought, except that the stubbornness and randy good looks will be tempered by sweetness and diplomacy now that there's been a little outside input."

The line of sunrise was widening, spreading the blocks of darkness apart, and Bailey felt it happen within herself, too. She'd really enjoyed her time in Bison City. And she was feeling a steadily mounting excitement about going back. All kinds of problems were at work now, but they didn't seem capable of quelling her enthusiasm for her visit.

She even felt happy enough to tease Jeff. "There were three whole days when you thought I was sweet."

"Mmm," he replied. "That was before you cut my heart out with a blunt machete and handed it to me."

Hurt feelings and acknowledged guilt pulled a shade down on her sunny mood. "I'm sorry," she said, emotion in her throat that felt like a pointed brick. "For three days we just had a good time, then...it all got too important. I hadn't expected that to happen."

"I'd have thought when your focus was freedom, you'd be expecting the unexpected all the time."

She gave him a dark look. "Well, I was new at it. I'd been free all of about three months. Apparently I had a lot to learn."

The seat belt lights dinged on, and the pilot announced that the flight attendants would be preparing for landing. Window shades were raised, flooding the cabin with light, and conversations began to hum.

Bailey combed her fingers through her hair and subsided into an unhappy little mound of pregnant woman.

JEFF HATED HIMSELF for having squashed her cheerful mood. His machete remark had been careless. He'd been determined when she'd left him that he wouldn't resent her for it, but when he'd found out she was pregnant, he'd felt justified in having feelings much stronger than resentment.

But she'd come with him—and though he knew she'd done it to keep the baby and not because she cared about him—it still provided him with what he wanted. At least for now.

He had to swallow all smart remarks from here on out if he was ever going to turn this in his favor for the long run.

"I apologize for that." He patted her knee. "I promise I'm not going to be needling you for two months. I guess I'm not quite over the surprise."

She gave him a suspicious side glance, then looked out the window at the bright blue sky. "It's all right. You didn't say anything that wasn't true. I don't think I was wrong to want my freedom, but I was wrong to forget that it means you can't indulge every fuzzy emotion."

"Fuzzy?"

"Fuzzy. The things you dream about under a warm blanket in a big cozy chair." She refocused on him. "When you're a child, it's a family like everyone else has. Mother *and* father, siblings, big dog, trips to the ice cream parlor and summer vacations."

Jeff had had all those. He didn't know whether to smile or frown. "You didn't have that?"

She shook her head. "My father died in a construction accident when I was four, and my mother was always in poor health. We never did much. I remember looking out my bedroom window all the time and wondering what was out there. When you're an adult," she continued, "you want all the same things, only now you have to provide them instead of just enjoy them, and the responsibility of making lifetime memories is scary. So you put it off.''

The plane shook for a few seconds, and she caught his arm in her two hands, her eyes darting around as though searching for the cause. ''What was that?''

''Just turbulence. Happens all the time right about here. Something to do with the mountains.''

They shook again, more violently this time. She held him a little more tightly. ''You're sure.''

He covered her hands clasped on his arm, enjoying her dependence, certain it wouldn't last long. ''I'm sure. Try to relax. Think about breakfast.''

''Okay.'' She closed her eyes as they shook a little more. ''Farmer's omelette with hash browns,'' she said. ''Whole wheat toast. Or eggs Benedict, maybe. Belgian waffle. I like those. With lots of cream.''

''Can you eat that stuff the way your stomach behaves?''

''I took my medicine. Ah!'' She put a hand to her stomach. ''Noelle doesn't like this shaking up, either.''

Jeff placed his hand beside hers. ''She kicked me earlier when you were asleep. Yep. There she is.'' He felt the smallest nudge against his palm, then another.

''Did you get any rest? I didn't mean to sprawl all over you.''

He laughed lightly. ''That's one of my most precious memories of you. The way you consider me your own personal mattress.''

THIS, SHE THOUGHT, huddled close to him, is my favorite memory of *you*—your solidity.

Somewhere under her awareness of the shaking plane, the somersaulting baby in her stomach and the uncertain future that lay ahead, she knew that holding on to something was no way to be free. But at that very moment what she wanted most was for herself and her baby to be safe.

So she held on, anyway, until they'd landed safely.

In Casper Jeff bought her breakfast as he'd promised. Then they picked up his blue van and started the three-and-a-half-hour drive up Interstate 25 to Interstate 90 and Bison City.

Bailey had forgotten how beautiful it was here. Big and open with none of the conveniences of home on every street corner because it could be fifty or sixty miles between street corners.

She felt just a little itchy for New York, for her drafting table, her computer with all its cyberspace bells and whistles, the cell phone and portable fax that she'd left at the studio.

Then she put thoughts of work out of her mind. She had to do this. She owed it to Jeff, and physically it would probably be very good for her and the baby.

Then, when the baby was born, they would come to an agreement like reasonable adults, and she would finally have her freedom. Well, whatever freedom one could reasonably expect with an infant in tow.

They made another stop for coffee and drove into Bison City just after noon.

The Way Station took up an entire block just behind the small but lively downtown area. It had once been the home of an eccentric millionaire friend of Samuel McIntyre, who entertained in great numbers. His friends would stay for weeks and months when travel depended upon the vagaries of the weather and a sometimes untrustworthy railroad schedule.

It was built in the style of a mountain lodge with whole logs and an entire wall of stone that rose three stories. Bailey was anxious to be inside again and realized it was because she wanted to show it to Noelle. She wanted the baby to feel what she'd felt the first time she'd walked into The Way Station. This place had a sense of home she'd never experienced before—even *at* home.

Jeff carried her bags and set them down to open the big double front doors for her.

Bailey walked inside, immediately assailed by the long beams of light coming in from the lounge's Palladian window and the wall of small-paned windows below it. The light fell onto a polished-oak floor, covered here and there with bright Indian rugs.

Set about the room were arrangements of twig chairs and settees with colorful cushions. In front of the fireplace sat an overstuffed beige sofa upon which had been tossed red, yellow, purple and blue throw cushions. Small tables around the room could be moved to accommodate business or coffee breaks.

She went to the fire in the fireplace and put her hands out to it. Above her, on a plain oak-slab mantel, was a copper kettle, a stylized metal sculpture of a buffalo, a leather box and a chafed silver pitcher holding a bunch of orange mums.

The small registration desk stood at the other end of the room and behind it was a familiar smiling face.

"Miss Dutton!" Maureen came around the desk to meet Bailey in the middle of the red, black and gold carpet. "You're back for another stay with us?" As she caught Bailey's outstretched hands, she looked over her pregnancy, then questioned with a smile, "Or are you Mrs. Somebody now?"

Maureen Wagner was medium in height and in her late sixties, with a porcelain complexion, despite a few wrinkles, gray eyes and a short cap of side-parted white hair that always looked perfect.

"No, still single," Bailey answered. She opened her mouth to offer an explanation, then wasn't sure what that explanation was. In New York she'd answered questions about her marital status and her baby with an honesty that wasn't precisely pride, but offered no excuses, either.

"We ran into each other in New York," Jeff said as he walked by with her bags, "and she's staying with me for a couple of months. Would you let the post office know?"

"Of course." Maureen took that news without blinking an eye. "Well, I'm so glad to see you, Miss Dutton. Jeff, your mail and messages are on your desk. Shall I get Sonny for those bags?"

"Thanks, but I've got them. Wait for me, Bailey. I'll come back to help you up the stairs."

"That's not neces—" She started after him when he turned and gave her what Josie used to call "the McIntyre stare." She claimed all her brothers used it. It was meant to ensure cooperation through intimidation.

Bailey scoffed at it and started up after him, anyway.

He put the bags down where he stood and caught her arm. "Fine," he said. "I'll come back for the bags."

"I'm very surefooted. I'll hold on to the railing."

"Bailey, your center of gravity is a foot out in front of you. You could take a header up the stairs or have the weight pitch you backward. Neither a scenario I'd like to see."

"Jeff..."

But he'd tuned out her protests and was leading her up the stairs.

"I'll send Sonny with the bags!" Maureen called after them.

When they reached the first floor, Peggy Jackson rounded the corner with her housekeeping cart. Physically, she was Maureen's opposite—middle thirties, dark-featured and short and plump in her crisp pink-and-white uniform. But she and Maureen were good friends, and she had the same warm and lively nature.

"Miss Dutton!" Peggy exclaimed. "How nice to have you back."

"Hi!" Bailey gave her a quick hug. "How are the kids? Did you ever get the bead out of Mitchell's navel?"

When Bailey had been here for the wedding, Peggy's six-year-old, Evie, had decorated her four-year-old brother with beads and glue while Peggy's husband, Eddy, had been napping on the sofa. They'd managed to remove all the beads, except the one in his navel. When Bailey left, Peggy had run out of solutions and was taking him to the Bison City Hospital.

Peggy made a face at Bailey. "Thank you. I'd managed to forget that. Getting it out was quite involved." She patted Bailey's stomach with a smile. "When did *this* happen? Eight months ago?"

"Seven," Bailey corrected, then realized what she'd done. Peggy cleaned Jeff's third-floor suite, as well as the other twenty rooms. She had to know when he had overnight company.

She saw the housekeeper's eyes swing instinctively to Jeff's, receiving his unembarrassed stare.

"Well, congratulations," Peggy said, giving her another hug. "All babies should be welcome. They just shouldn't all be allowed to grow up to play with beads and glue. Call me if you need anything."

"Who else do you know?" Jeff asked, helping Bailey the rest of the way up the stairs. "You were only here three days."

"We all got to chatting the afternoon you left with Matt and Alex to decorate Justin's car for the honeymoon. They're great ladies."

He nodded. "I've always thought so. I just didn't know you knew them."

She smiled, breathing a little hard as they reached the third floor. "I'm sure there's a lot we don't know about each other."

"That's what we're here to discover." He pushed open the double glass doors that shut off the third floor from outside noise and ushered Bailey through. They entered his suite through a small carpeted foyer decorated with a hall table and a potted palm.

The last time he'd brought her here, she remembered, walking into the dark-blue-and-white living room, they'd been tired from the wedding and high on the camaraderie of family and friends and too many toasts made with Dom Perignon.

She'd looked forward to an evening in his company, then he'd built a fire, given her a look that turned everything she knew upside down and kissed her.

And then the tone of the evening changed. Friendship deepened into romance, romance had turned to passion, and that heady threesome had led them into the most astonishing night.

He thought love had resulted, but she hadn't let it happen. She was sure she'd just responded to his welcoming nature, to the confidence about him that made her feel at peace, to the wonderful warmth of the McIntyres, the cozy decor of The Way Station and the charm of the town and its people.

She felt that same comfort enfold her in the suite's living room with its warm white walls, bare oak floor, dark beams and the comfortable furnishings upholstered in various patterns of dark blue and white. There were red and yellow highlights here and there and a table with a blue-and-white-checkered cloth that was covered with memorabilia from the ranch.

She felt the tug of connection and tried hard to dispel it.

"You can have the second bedroom in the back," Jeff said, leading her through the living room into a small hallway and the room at the opposite end from his.

It was decorated in rose and white with a white crocheted covering on a brass bed. There were straw hats and old framed advertisements on the wall. A long window looked out onto the paved parking area below, then past that to a thick but spindly aspen woods. The leaves were rusty brown now and starting to fall.

She felt a homesickness for New York, yet she appreciated the beauty of her surroundings. She felt a little as though her life was slowing to a stop. Could she do this? Two months of beauty, but nothing else?

JEFF WATCHED BAILEY put one hand to the window as she looked out. There was a sort of desperation in the gesture, he thought, a kind of imprisoned look.

"When I sold the house in the Hamptons," he said quickly, hoping to relieve her mind if she was worried about two months with nothing to do, "I packed up and shipped home a workroom I had there. You can have the drafting table and the taboret when they arrive. We can put them right where you're standing."

She stepped back, as though picturing the things there. She seemed pleasantly surprised and even brightened a little. "That'd be nice. I've been working on a line to eventually start my own house. I brought my designs with me."

They heard what sounded like a collision in the living room, a crash, then a string of mild but sincere profanity.

Jeff smiled thinly. "I'd say Sonny's here with your bags."

Sonny was tall and thin and somewhere in his early seventies. He'd come with the hotel, as had Maureen, and he continued to work despite arthritis and poor eyesight because he had nothing in the world but his friends at The Way Station.

Jeff kept him on despite his depth perception problems and his tendency to collide with things and break them, because he didn't have the heart to do otherwise. And he knew Sonny was grateful for the job.

Jeff hurried into the living room to find Sonny sprawled over a hassock, Bailey's bags scattered around him. He hurried to help the old man up.

"You all right, Sonny? Did you hurt anything?"

Sonny tugged at his jacket while Jeff brushed him off. "Not even my pride. We all know I'm an arthritic old geezer, so it removes the pressure of pretending I'm not. Thank you, Mr. McIntyre." Sonny noticed Bailey and beamed as he extended his hand to her. "Why, Miss Dutton! What a nice surprise. You're back to stay with us?" His eyes went to her pregnancy, but unlike the women at The Way Station, he politely pretended not to notice. Just as he hadn't commented on the fact that he'd brought Bailey's bags to Jeff's suite rather than to a guest room. "How nice."

Bailey shook his hand. "It's nice to see you, Sonny," she said, then leaned closer to him and asked, lowering her voice, "Have you told Maureen how you feel yet, or are you still fixing her car and bringing her buttermilk bars from the bakery and pretending you're just her friend?"

Sonny blushed, something Jeff had never seen before. He watched in astonishment as his bellman lost the poise he'd maintained even after falling over the hassock. Sonny ran a finger inside the collar of his uniform shirt. "Miss Dutton..." he said in a weak voice.

"It's all right, Sonny." Bailey gave him an apologetic hug. "I didn't mean to upset you. I was just curious. I thought you might have a ring on her finger by now."

He glanced uncomfortably at Jeff. "She's a widow with a nice house and everything else she needs. What would she need with me?"

"Maybe that's a question you should think about," Bailey suggested.

Sonny frowned at her, then turned to Jeff, clearly trying to reestablish equanimity after Bailey's invasion of his personal space. "Anything else I can do for you, Mr. McIntyre?"

Normally Jeff wouldn't have asked him to make two trips to the third floor, but he looked as though he needed something to do. Jeff handed him his car keys. "My bag is still in the trunk. Why don't you take your lunch break, then bring it up?"

"Yes, sir."

When the door closed behind Sonny, Jeff picked up Bailey's bags and carried them into her room. "You mean, Sonny's sweet on Maureen?" he asked, placing the bags on her bed.

She held on to the brass footboard and watched him with a sort of pitying indulgence. "How could you not have noticed? He brings her treats from the bakery, he's there if she needs help with anything...."

"But he does that for me, too."

"Does he watch you from across the lobby with his heart in his eyes? I don't think so."

"For a woman who's determined to remain free," he observed, carrying her suit bag to hang it up in the empty closet, "you sure make a point of knowing what's going on in everyone else's life. Don't tell me Sonny was involved in your quiet afternoon with Maureen and Peggy?"

She smiled. "He ran to the bakery to get us cookies to go with our tea, but he didn't stay to have it with us. It's just something I noticed. He's very attentive to her, hangs on her every word—" she sighed "—and worships her from afar."

Jeff came back to the bed and took up her place at the footpost as she unlocked her suitcases. "Getting that involved with people on such short acquaintance is going to make inroads into your freedom, isn't it?"

She threw back the top of a pink-and-gray brocade case. A pair of woolly red ankle-high slippers with fleece lining sat right on top. "Not at all. I just noticed, I'm not involved."

He picked up the slippers to examine the soft soles. "When you ask about people's children and the crushes they think no one knows about, you do more than notice. You care. Caring is involvement."

She reclaimed the slippers. "Caring about acquaintances doesn't take the same toll on your peace of mind as...romantic caring."

"In your romantic caring you also are cared about," he said. "Then it doesn't take a toll on you at all. It doubles your power."

She closed her eyes and shook her head. "Do you have to take issue with every statement I make?"

He smiled. "Only when you're wrong. And I'm

sorry, Bailey, but you're wrong a lot. And don't wear those." He pointed to the slippers. "You'll kill yourself on these floors. We'll find you a pair with soles." He started for the door.

"Then they won't feel like slippers," she complained.

"And you won't feel like you've fallen on your backside. I'll see what we've got for lunch."

BAILEY CLUTCHED her snuggly slippers to her and thought about how wonderful they felt on her feet. Cold feet were always a problem for her, but now that she was pregnant and it was fall, the problem intensified.

He was probably right about the slick bottoms of her slippers on the hardwood floor. She'd had carpet in her New York apartment.

She tossed the slippers aside, put away everything from the case, then replaced the slippers and put the case under the bed, thinking that in all her involvement with Jeff's employees she'd still felt perfectly complete....

But a few words from Jeff about slippers and she felt as though the freedom she so prized had been severely compromised. But, of course it had. Slippers aside, she was here with him instead of home in New York.

She patted the baby consolingly. "Don't worry, Noelle," she said. "We'll stay long enough for you to meet him, long enough for him to make whatever arrangements he feels he has to for you, then we're out of here."

Noelle gave her a good, swift kick.

Chapter Four

Bailey scanned the living room for her purse, in search of her medication, and found Jeff pulling things out of an overhead cupboard with one hand while holding a cordless phone to his ear with the other.

His end of the conversation became discernible as she spotted her purse on the table that separated the kitchen from the living room and went toward it.

"How long do you estimate it would take?" he asked. Seeing her coming toward him, he took a wedge of orange from a small plate on the counter and handed it to her.

She loved oranges. Had he remembered that? His eyes told her he had.

Thank you, she mouthed.

He nodded. "Two weeks," he said to the person on the other end of the line. "You're sure. That sounds optimistic. We're talking about a three-story structure."

A firm rap sounded on the front door of the suite. Bailey, on her way back to her room, turned to

Jeff and raised an eyebrow in question, pointing to the door.

He nodded that she should answer it. Into the phone he said, "Yes, I'll be here all afternoon."

Bailey pulled open the door and found Josie standing there, a pizza box balanced on the palm of her hand. Josie's dark eyes widened in shock. She studied Bailey in complete confusion for a moment, then squealed and threw her arms around her, pizza box and all.

Bailey drew her inside and closed the door. She took the box from her and placed it on the nearby coffee table.

"Josie! It is *so* good to see you. You look wonderful! Huge, but wonderful!" Josie was four or five inches taller than Bailey, but her pregnancy protruded considerably, though she still managed to look elegant. She wore jeans and a thick white sweater with a rolled neck. Bailey, at five foot three, felt suddenly very stubby.

"What are you doing in Bison City?" Josie demanded, grinning from ear to ear.

But before Bailey could answer, Josie, in the act of looking her up and down, stopped and stared at the mound of her stomach as had every pair of eyes she'd encountered so far today.

"I didn't know you were pregnant! Why didn't you tell me? Who's the—" She stopped short, apparently finding the answer to all her questions when her eyes swung to the kitchen where her brother was still on the phone.

Jeff blew her a kiss.

Josie turned to Bailey, her eyes huge, her mouth

twitching in indecision between a smile and an "Oh!" of surprise. "No!"

Bailey nodded. "Jeff's. Yes."

"Well…I thought you liked each other, but then Jeff never talked about you." Hands on her hips, she turned to frown at her brother. "He never mentioned a baby."

He put his finger to his lips, silently asking her to lower her voice.

"I hadn't told him," Bailey confessed, now the target of that frown as Josie turned back to her. She went toward the sofa, her back suddenly tired. "Well, I knew it just couldn't be, between us, and he was pretty angry, and when I got home and found out a few weeks later… I didn't want to obligate either one of us to anything."

Josie sat beside her on the sofa, her frown still in place. "Well, I can imagine how that went over when he found you. How *did* he find you? Did he look you up in New York after all?"

Bailey explained about their accidental meeting in the studio at the advertising firm.

"Oh, my God."

"Yeah."

Josie looked into Bailey's eyes as though searching for answers. "Did he make an ugly scene? All my brothers tend to get…loud when they're not pleased."

"No, he was quite civilized," Bailey said in his defense, though she wasn't sure what would have happened if she hadn't gotten sick when she did, forcing him to take her back to her place.

"Then, I don't understand. I know how much you

wanted to get to New York. How'd he get you to come back here?''

Bailey smiled grimly. ''Intimidation.'' She told Josie about their disagreement over her return and their argument over the custody issue.

Josie looked less sympathetic than Bailey had hoped. She patted Bailey's hand and said philosophically, ''You're having a McIntyre, sweetie. Keeping them close is family policy.''

''She's half Dutton.''

''Well, we'll have to morph you into a McIntyre, won't we? Then there won't be any question.'' Josie seemed aware of something else suddenly and asked, ''She? That's wonderful. I wrote you that I'm having a boy.'' She looked her over with a critical eye. ''We must be due about the same time. Last week in December?''

''Christmas Day.''

''Wow! Remember how we used to lie in the dark in the dorm on rainy nights and talk about me coming to New York with you, and we'd both marry rich executives and raise our kids together and meet twice a week for lunch?''

Bailey smiled fondly over the thought. They'd been so convinced it could happen. Then Bailey's mother had gotten sick, and Josie had come home to Bison City, and all their dreams had dissolved.

''Well, now we can still do it,'' Josie said. ''Only here in Bison City. And without the rich executive husbands.''

''Rich executive husbands?'' Jeff asked, finished with his call. He came to stand before them and leaned down to kiss Josie on the cheek. ''Whose?''

"Ours." Josie traced a finger in the air between herself and Bailey. "It was a college-dorm dream of ours to marry rich executives and raise our kids together."

"I see. So, you're leaving Justin?"

Josie laughed. "We may have to alter the original plan a little. I drove by to see if you were back yet, spotted your car in the lot and picked up a pizza for us in the hope you hadn't had lunch yet. And what a wonderful surprise!"

Josie hugged Bailey again. "I can't believe she's here!" She smiled up at Jeff. "I understand you bullied her into coming."

"That I did," he admitted with no sign of guilt.

Josie grinned gleefully. "Well, good for you. I'm so happy to see her, I can't stand it. And she's having my niece! This is where she should be."

Jeff patted Josie's head. "That's what I thought. You ladies chat, and I'll get plates and napkins."

THEY WERE COMPARING discomfort notes when Jeff returned, and he simply sat back and listened, enjoying the glow they exuded in each other's company if not the subject of their discussion.

"And you can help with the Bison City baby contest," Josie said after reeling out a long list of all the things the two of them could do over the next few months. She licked her fingers, then wiped them on a napkin.

"Baby contest?" Bailey asked. She was still working on her first piece of pizza. "Oh, you mean one of those first-baby-of-the-year things, where you get diapers and linens?"

"Sort of." Josie explained in happy detail the contest she had developed to benefit the hospital.

Bailey offered the same argument Jeff had raised before he'd left for New York. "You can't make much money on the number of pregnant women in the county. I mean, how many can there be?"

"Thirty-one," Josie replied.

Bailey's eyes widened. "You're kidding. In this county alone? You people have entirely too much time on your hands."

Jeff leaned back with a can of cola. "This is Wyoming, where the Great Plains meet the Rocky Mountains. Our lowest elevation is 3100 feet. Home of the brontosaurus and the contemporary Western male. We don't do anything in a small way."

Josie rolled her eyes at him, then said to Bailey with a reluctant nod, "Actually, he's right. Big ideas abound here. And you know what most men think about first."

She did. But as she recalled, when Jeff had thought about it that wedding weekend, it had been tops on her mind, too. But she didn't want to think about it now. That's what had nipped her freedom in the bud.

"Well, even with thirty-one, Josie, that's only 155 dollars. And even a dollar a ticket to guess the time of birth… What are you hoping to buy the hospital?"

Josie ticked the list off on her fingers. "Books, games, toys, teddy bears, some other stuff. This is a small town. We're trying to stick with what we can reasonably expect to accomplish. Jeff's going to help us promote." She turned to him expectantly. "Did you come up with anything on the plane?"

He pointed to Bailey, clearly mulling over Josie's

idea while popping a piece of pepperoni into her mouth. "I brought you one of New York's great minds in design."

Bailey refocused on him at that. "*Clothing* design," she emphasized.

"Design is design," he said, gathering up empty plates. "If your mind works in those terms, you should be able to make it apply to anything."

"You're the advertising expert. You're supposed to know what reaches people and how to manipulate what they feel and how they respond."

That touched a sore spot. "Ideally," he corrected, taking her crumpled napkin from her, "I try to understand people first, then explain the product in clear and honest terms so that the buyer can make an informed choice without being manipulated."

"Well, you understand people," Josie said to him, reaching up for his arm to get herself off the sofa. "You should be able to make this work." She indicated Bailey. "Between the great design mind and the great people person, you should come up with a brilliant plan to present our ideas before the public."

Jeff went to the kitchen, put the things he carried on the counter, then returned to see his sister off. "You've spent entirely too much time with politicians. You're beginning to sound like a spin doctor."

She laughed lightly. "Justin does bring a lot of work home. Well, got to go."

Jeff wrapped his arms around her. "Thanks for the pizza, Jose."

"Sure." She turned to say goodbye to Bailey, who was struggling to get off the sofa.

Jeff went to offer Bailey a hand up.

"Whew!" she said. "Remind me never to sit there again."

Josie hugged Bailey.

"I'll walk you down the stairs," Jeff said, pointing Bailey to the suite. "I'll be right back. Why don't you take a nap?"

"Because I'm not tired."

"Then sit somewhere and put that design mind to work on Josie's project."

Bailey groaned and closed the door.

Josie stopped Jeff at the top of the stairs. "Have you called Matt and Alex about Bailey? Or Mom and Dad?"

"No, I haven't. We just got home."

"Can I?" she asked with unabashed eagerness.

"By all means. I'm sure you can make it far more dramatic than I could."

She held on to him as they started down. "You weren't really rotten to her to make her come here, were you?"

He'd always been honest with Josie. "I may have been."

She turned to frown at him. "She said you intimidated her, but she wasn't specific."

"Will you watch where you're going, please?" He heard the defensive quality of his own voice. "She was trying to tell me that she didn't want anything from me and she didn't want me in the baby's life. So I threatened to fight her for custody."

"Jeff," she scolded quietly. "I know she was wrong to keep the baby from you, but she's had a tough time. She was so smart and enthusiastic, and she had such big ideas. But she gave up everything to take care of her mom. She was very philosophical about it, and she never whined or complained, but I can imagine what it must have been like for her when she was finally able to do with her life what she'd wanted to do all that time.''

They crossed the second floor landing and continued down. ''I can understand that. But I can't understand her trying to steal my child from me.''

''I don't think that was her intention.''

''Well, that would have been the result had I not run into her at Braverman's.''

''Okay, but now that you have her here, can you get that granite look off your face and just let her get comfortable and feel secure? She never had that, you know. Her dad was gone, her mother was never well, so there was never anyone for her to run to...except me.'' She grinned. ''And you know how flaky I am. I was so spoiled, I could sympathize, but I couldn't relate.''

''What granite look?'' he demanded.

''This granite look.'' As they walked out onto the street, she made a face that looked like something out of Dr. Frankenstein's laboratory. Then she was herself again ''Matt and Alex do it, too. I think you learned it from Dad. It's the I-know-what's-best-for-you-and-I'm-going to scare-you-into-doing-it look. I'm telling you, it's not going to scare her, it's just going to tick her off, so stop it.''

He walked her to her red Neon. ''I am not trying to scare her. But I want her to know I'm serious about taking responsibility for the baby and being part of her life.''

"Then do it with kindness." She hugged him again and got in behind the wheel. She just fit.

"Why don't you mind your business?" he asked amiably.

She put the key in the ignition and squinted up at him against the sun. "If I minded my business," she asked, "how would you know what to do?"

"I coped for seven years before you came along."

"If you call fighting with Matt and Alex coping. I tell you, if anyone needs my interference—" she smiled and considered another word "—my contribution…it's Matt. What are we going to do about him?"

"Let him be," he advised firmly. "Grief's different for everyone. Give him time."

"Mom's worried about him."

"We're all worried about him, but if he knew we were even talking about what to do for him, he'd disown all of us. Say hi to Justin."

"Okay."

He closed her door.

"You be nice to Bailey!" she shouted at him through the window.

He waved as she drove away.

BAILEY PUT HER THINGS AWAY and tidied up the kitchen. Jeff called her from the lobby to tell her he had a minor crisis to take care of and he'd be tied up until dinner.

She toyed with the idea of going through her sketches for her own line in the hope of generating new ideas, but she was too edgy to think. She still felt as though the contents of her brain were being tumbled like dice in a cage. And that was an appropriate metaphor, she thought. Two ideas in her brain right now would be a lot.

She put on her jacket and went out to explore Bison City. Maureen was busy at the desk, and the door to Jeff's office was closed, so she left without explaining to anyone, certain she'd be back in less than an hour. As she remembered, there wasn't that much of the little town to explore.

It was a perfect fall day, though a little colder than New York for early November. The sun was bright, the sky blue, the mountains around them purple and craggy.

Bison City's downtown, one block from The Way Station, seemed to be composed of modern architecture embracing and extending the one-block-long original main street with its squarish false fronts and shingled-roofed sidewalk.

There was a tack shop next to a software vendor, a feed and grain store next to a theater showing *Mission to Alpha Centauri,* a flower shop in a little house that had probably been on the edge of town in the old days, next to a professional building with an orthodontist, a stock broker and a satellite dish company.

Bailey had to smile. Who said small towns were stuck in the past? This one seemed to have learned to hold on to it while still continuing to move ahead.

She stopped in a fabric shop, wondering how she'd missed it the last time she was here. Of course, the wedding had occupied her time and focus then.

She was immediately charmed and fascinated by hundreds of patterned cottons and chintzes. She itched to buy, then remembered her sewing machine was in New York.

It didn't matter, she reasoned. She could take it home with her. But she knew herself. If she had fabric, she would be hemming it into scarves—anything to be able to work with it.

Then she experienced a stroke of genius! A baby quilt for Josie! The small project could be done by hand in the two months until Josie was due.

Having a valid reason to buy revved her enthusiasm until she was walking back and forth among the bolts of fabric, matching and contrasting colors, coordinating patterns, narrowing her choices.

Unable to decide between a collection of pink fabrics and an array of green ones, she decided on both. She might as well make one for herself while she was at it.

She bought thread, batting and simple polka-dot fabrics for the underside of the quilt. She could hardly see her way out the door. Once on the sidewalk, she was shocked to discover that the sun had set and dusk lay over the now-busy downtown, and lights were on everywhere as merchants and shoppers alike hurried home to dinner.

She walked quickly toward the commercial area's only stoplight, then crossed the street and headed for The Way Station. So much for being back in under an hour, but fabric stores were always fatal to her efficiency.

A BOOKING CRISIS handled and rescheduled, Jeff went upstairs just before five with Josie's advice playing back in his mind. "Be kind."

Not that he'd been *un*kind. He's just been a little insistent. But then he'd been right, so that made it acceptable. He laughed at himself as he imagined how Josie would react to that reasoning.

He let himself into the suite. Silence greeted him in the empty living room. He peered into the kitchen. No one there.

"Bailey?" he called.

When there was no answer, he crossed the living room to the bedrooms and found that hers had been left open, but she wasn't there.

An ugly, alarming suspicion crossed his mind and he yanked her closet door open. But all her things were there. He felt instant relief but it was only momentary. She hadn't wanted to come, he reasoned with himself. She'd have left *without* her things if it had meant she could get away.

He stormed back into the living room and called the desk. It took Maureen several rings to answer. "Front desk."

"Maureen, it's Jeff. Is Bailey down there?"

There was a moment's surprised silence. "Ah... no. I don't think so. I mean, I haven't seen her. I'm a little busy, but I can have Sonny check the dining room."

"No, I'll take care of it." He put the phone down, a little surprised at the quickening of his heartbeat. And it wasn't entirely temper. She was stubborn enough to have left, but she was small and prone to being sick, and all alone in a dark and unfamiliar place. Where did he start looking for her?

A loud knock on the door interrupted his anguished thoughts. Actually, it didn't sound as much like a knock as a kick. As he headed toward it, he heard a faint voice call, ''Jeff?''

Bailey's voice.

He yanked the door open, angry words on the tip of his tongue, but it wasn't Bailey. At least the first layer wasn't Bailey. It was paper bags. They marched past him into the living room, positioned themselves in front of the sofa, then free-fell onto the cushions.

Bailey stood there in a dark blue jacket. As he shed the anxious possibilities of a moment ago, he noticed absently that her nose was red, her cheeks were pink, and her eyes and lips were smiling.

''You didn't tell me Bison City has a fabric store!'' she said excitedly, reaching into one of the bags to pull out fabric and drape it over the back of the sofa. ''I couldn't believe it! I'd almost talked myself out of buying anything, since I don't even have a sewing machine, but then I thought about making a quilt for Josie. I can do that by hand, you know, and there's plenty of—'' A glance up at him as she delved into the bag stopped her midsentence, and she focused on his face. ''What?'' she asked, surprise mixed with trepidation in her eyes.

''You might have told me you were going.'' God. He sounded like his mother in a snit.

''Your office door was closed,'' she said reasonably, ''and Maureen was busy. When you called, you said you had some kind of crisis, and I didn't think—''

He pointed a finger at himself as he walked around the sofa toward her. ''I called. I didn't leave you to just wonder where I was when I didn't come back.''

''I thought I was only going to be an hour or so.''

She continued to speak quietly as she unzipped her jacket. She looked a little like a large blueberry with arms and legs. "I didn't realize—"

Jeff struggled to find his customary easy balance in a crisis but couldn't strike it. Josie's advice was completely forgotten.

"Well, it's time you *did* realize," he interrupted. "I know you'd like nothing better now that you're free of family, but you are not in this world alone. And for the next two months at least, you owe me the courtesy of letting me know where you are. You don't just take off in the dark!" His voice rose at the end, balance still eluding him.

He saw her temper ignite. "It's not even 5:00 p.m.! I don't think street gangs—if they did exist in the mountains of Wyoming—are even out yet!"

That response only served to deepen his own anger.

"You don't know your way around here, and my concern isn't for street gangs, but for traffic. You're wearing dark blue at night. A car wouldn't have been able to see you!"

She spread her arms. "What? I'm not a big enough target?"

"Bailey—"

"Jeffrey!" She implored the heavens with raised arms. "What do I need to know to get around a town that's three blocks long? What is the matter with you?"

He turned away from her and went into the kitchen, wondering how in the hell he was supposed to save face now. He'd just shouted at her for absolutely nothing because he'd thought she'd left—and she hadn't.

He turned around again and found her right behind him, hands on her hips—or where her hips would have been but for her belly—and a look of stupefaction on her face.

He struggled for words that would leave him a modicum of pride while still making things clear to her.

"It was dark," he said reasonably, "and I had no idea where you were. I don't think it would infringe so dramatically on your independence to ask that next time you take off for hours, you tell me where you're going."

"You—"

"I know." He raised a quieting hand. "I was dealing with a crisis. But you can consider yourself and the baby more important to me than a closed office door."

She folded her arms, clearly still indignant. The pose atop her round stomach was almost comical. "I will not answer to you for my every move. I'm an adult, and though you seem to be convinced to the contrary, I can take care of myself, the baby and whatever might come at me in the dark in downtown Bison City."

"I'm sure you can," he said patiently. "All I ask is that you let me know where you are while you're doing it."

DURING THE LAST FEW MINUTES, Bailey's emotions had ranged from confusion to anger and were now moving hesitantly toward enlightenment.

He'd been worried. She found that enormously annoying, but also…touching. She'd been too young to remember her father worrying about her, and her mother had usually been too ill to worry about anyone but herself.

"I can cope," she said placatingly.

He caught her shoulders, his grip tightening just a little. "Bailey, try to understand this. I know you're intelligent and capable. It has nothing to do with that. But you're carrying my baby. You and the baby are in a somewhat delicate condition and it would relieve my mind a great deal just to know where you are. Think of it as *my* weakness and not yours. All right?"

Well. That put it all in perspective for her. He was worried about the baby. Of course. That was the reason she was here—not because she was Bailey, but because Bailey was carrying Noelle.

She nodded. "Okay. Sure," she said and turned to gather up her things and put them away.

He caught her arm. "No," he said. "I know what you're thinking, and you're wrong. If I didn't have feelings for you, you wouldn't be pregnant today— at least not with *my* baby. Anyway, it's time to stop thinking of yourself as a loner. You're not even alone in your own body anymore."

Bailey had long ago accepted that. And she knew he'd cared about her when Noelle had been conceived. But she felt reasonably sure if there'd been some way to separate her from the baby when he'd found her, he'd have done so.

"Yeah, right," she said. "If you'd had any obstetric skills, you'd have left me in New York and brought just the baby to Wyoming.''

She watched his attempt to be reasonable with her dissolve into simple frustration. ''Well, I didn't, and here we all are. For a woman who insists she can cope, you're doing your damnedest not to.'' He turned back to the kitchen. ''Give me a couple of minutes and I'll get something together for dinner.''

She was suddenly very tired, and her back ached from all those hours poring over bolts of fabric. She conceded grudgingly to herself that he was right. He shouldn't have yelled at her, but she should have left a message or a note.

She went to the bags she'd left on the sofa and pulled out a small thermal brown sack. She put it on the counter beside him. ''I bought a roasted chicken and a container of pasta salad at the supermarket deli on my way home. I thought you might still be dealing with your crisis.''

She could see that he didn't want to smile, but he allowed himself to, anyway. ''Now, that was thoughtful,'' he praised. ''A team-player sort of approach to dinner. If you could just apply that concept to letting me know where you are...''

She felt herself wanting to smile and couldn't understand why. She withheld it, but it made her mouth twitch. ''Maybe you could just get me a beeper.''

She saw his eyes focus on the twitch, then raise to her eyes. ''Now you're being smart. And I don't mean that in a good way. Go wash your hands before I decide not to share this with you.''

She went to gather up her packages. "I'm not worried about that," she said.

"Why not?"

"You wouldn't be setting much of a team-player example, would you?"

Chapter Five

Bailey went to bed early, and Jeff went downstairs to make sure all was quiet for the night. The swing-shift clerk, a college kid taking a year off to earn enough money to go back, looked up from a psychology text.

"Hi, Mr. McIntyre," he said. "Have a good trip?"

Jeff nodded. "Glad to be home, though, David. How's everything out here?"

"Quiet."

"Good."

Jeff went into his office to clear away some of the paperwork that had accumulated while he'd been gone, then returned to the suite just before eleven. He heard quiet noises from Bailey's room.

He went to the hallway and listened. Her door was closed, but through it he heard creaking and the crash of something to the floor. He knocked on the door. "Bailey, are you all right?"

There was a moment's silence, then the door opened. She stood there in a long blue-and-white flannel nightgown, her hair atumble, her eyes tired and betraying pain.

"Would you be all right if you had five little toes stuck in between your ribs?" She smiled wryly. "I'm fine. But I guess the trip upset our little Irish step dancer. She doesn't want to sleep, and my back's killing me. I was trying to get up and I accidentally knocked over the clock radio."

"Would a back rub help?" he asked, fully expecting to be rejected.

But she considered the suggestion, then said with a widening of the wry smile, "I have nine hundred dollars in my savings account and some stock. You can have all of it if you can make her settle down."

"She's a McIntyre. You're asking a lot."

She frowned as she pulled the door all the way open. "You keep forgetting that she's half me."

"No, I'm not." He followed her to the bed, picked up the clock and replaced it on the bedside table. The relentless second hand continued to work as though nothing had happened. "It's just that in this case it doesn't help. Lie down on your sto— Oh, you can't, can you?"

"Sort of." She lay on her side, bunched a pillow up under her upper body and leaned halfway over it.

Jeff made himself block out the impression of a soft bed and a fragrant woman and remembered that he was trying to help in a situation where he could usually do very little.

"Where's the pain?" he asked practically, sitting right beside her bottom. He put the soft curve out of his mind.

"Everywhere," she said with a small groan. "Her

feet are right about here.'' She rubbed at a spot on her right side. ''But the base of my spine hurts. I guess I spent too long on my feet at the fabric store.''

He put a hand to the small of her back. ''Right here?''

He felt the slightest reaction in her, a little jump that might have been surprise or pain.

''Yeah,'' she said after a moment.

''Did that hurt?''

''No,'' she replied quietly.

So. It had been surprise. Not surprise that he'd touched her, because she'd asked him to. But surprise that it affected her, perhaps?

He began to rub gently. In the slightly awkward position beside her, he had to throw an arm over her in order to work in comfort. He felt the stiff tension in her back and the tight tuck of her legs.

''I'm sorry about this evening.'' The words came out of her in a breathless little rush. Then she uttered a sound that was half gasp, half groan. ''God, that feels good.''

He continued to stroke up and down from the middle of her back to the bottom of her spine. ''It's all right,'' he said. ''I'm sure we'll find a lot to argue about over the next couple of months.''

She wriggled a little and groaned again. ''I don't regret arguing with you,'' she clarified. ''But I do regret scaring you. It's been a while since it mattered to anyone where I was going.''

He ignored her qualifying remarks in the interest of peace and broadened his stroke to include the side of her waist where she claimed the baby's toes were separating her ribs. "You think the pepperoni made her restless?"

"I think she was restless when she was just two little cells," she replied. "Supposedly a calm mother makes for a calm baby, but this child's had my body in upheaval—literally—and, of course, I was worried about—"

She stopped.

He guessed what she'd been about to say. She was worried about supporting her, caring for her, being everything she needed. But this back rub was about trying to calm her, so he said nothing.

Bailey stretched her legs out, beginning to relax. "You've let several perfectly good I-told-you-so opportunities slip right by," she teased. "I can't believe you have nothing to say."

"Nothing slips by me," he corrected. "And when I have something to say, I usually say it. Right now I'm concentrating on getting the kinks out of your back. I don't remember you being this tense."

"I've had a lot on my mind." She spoke in a tone that discouraged questions, so he simply kept up his work without comment.

He knew the moment she became putty in his hands. She stretched her arms up along the coverlet as the tension left her. He began to work exclusively where the baby was perched, and she leaned back against his thigh, giving him easier access. He moved her pillow under her head.

It amazed him that he could touch her with such control. His memories of this woman were composed of hot passion and righteous anger, but all he could feel now as he ran his hands over their baby was tenderness and possession.

He rubbed over her stomach to the protrusion of her belly button, then back again to her side, over and over. Then suddenly he felt movement under his hand like the sweep of a foot, as though the baby had changed positions.

Bailey expelled a long, slow sigh of relief. "You did it! I can't believe you did it. Did you feel that? She moved. Now she's sitting on my bladder, but that's easier to deal with."

Laughing, she put her hand over his on her stomach. "Thank you. I can't tell you how much better that feels. I rub her all the time and she never moves for me."

"She probably heard you offer me nine hundred dollars and stock options and is hoping to get her hands on it by cooperating."

"You think so?"

"According to Josie, the baby can hear now. She made Justin stop swearing. That's hard for a newspaper man in politics."

She smiled lazily. "What do you suppose she wants worth nine hundred dollars?"

"A horse," he replied. "A bay with a sweet disposition and a love of speed."

Silence fell between them, and he knew the peaceful, fanciful interlude was over.

"Where would I put a horse in New York?" she asked after a moment.

He shrugged a shoulder. "Got me. I guess you and she will have to work that out."

She propped herself up on an elbow, and he braced

himself for an argument, but she just frowned. Then she tried to sit up, but floundered dangerously on the soft mattress.

He stood, turned her gently so that her head was aimed at the pillows, then lifted her and placed her among them. He reclaimed the pillow she'd leaned on and dropped it beside her, then pulled up the blankets.

She accidentally kicked his hand as she tucked her feet under the covers. It was like making contact with a block of ice. He caught the foot in one hand and rubbed it with the other. "I forgot this about you," he said, reaching for the other foot and doing the same. "Your feet seem to have their own weather system going, spring or fall. You about put me into a cryogenic state with them the night we spent together. Did you bring any socks?"

She shook her head.

At his answering frown, she explained pointedly, "I packed in rather a hurry," she said. "And most of my clothes are for working. I have lots of stockings and one pair of cotton Mickey Mouse socks I wear with flats." She pulled her foot away. "I won't be putting my feet on you tonight, so you needn't worry."

He pulled the blankets over her and left the room.

Good work, she told herself as she sank into the pillows. *He gives you a back rub that was indeed worth nine hundred dollars and you get snippy. Without thanking him for going out of his way after what had to have been a long day for him, too.*

But she'd apparently underestimated his ability to

take her guff. He was back in a minute with a large woolly lump of something white. Socks!

He peeled them apart, tossed the blankets back at the foot of the bed and forced them onto her feet. The socks had red ribbing at the tops and reached all the way to her knees. They were soft and thick and felt instantly wonderful.

He replaced the blankets and tucked them in again. ''Only problem with them is, you have to take them off when you get up or you'll fall. Priority number two tomorrow is to buy you slippers with skid-proof soles.''

She raised an eyebrow. ''What's the first priority?''

''Taking you to Bison City's very own obstetrician. She's new, but Josie swears you'll like her.''

''But...don't we need an appointment?''

He nodded. ''I made one this afternoon.''

''I thought you were dealing with a crisis?''

''I thought I told you your needs would always take precedence over a crisis. Anyway. It took me all of five minutes. We're due at 10:00 a.m.''

She hated having decisions made for her. She wanted to be annoyed that he'd made an appointment for her without telling her, but it wasn't as though she had a choice of OB-GYNs out here. And it wasn't as though she'd been around to be consulted.

The wisest course at seven months along was to establish a working relationship right away with the doctor who would guide her to term and deliver her baby.

All those excuses lined up in order, she decided it was all right to experience this little glow. She'd never been taken care of before. It wasn't so much that she liked it as that it was simply a novel experience.

"Thank you," she said politely. "And thank you for the back rub. You were worth big money and stock options tonight."

He came to the head of the bed, braced his hands on his knees and leaned over her. "Actually," he said, "I'm considered priceless pretty much most of the time. Anything else you need?"

To be far, far away from you, she thought as she looked up into his blue eyes. But she was suddenly very relaxed, very comfortable among all the pillows, and her feet were wonderfully warm. At the moment she wouldn't have moved even an inch had the curtains been on fire.

"No, thank you. Good night."

"Okay. Call me if you need anything." He turned off her bedside light and left the room.

THE HOSPITAL WAS VERY SMALL, just three rooms where Jeff said old Doc Wilson had practiced since the McIntyres were children. He'd retired two years earlier and now Dave Gardner, a GP who'd come from Cheyenne, treated everything from splinters to broken bones.

But it was Dr. Elizabeth Lee who gave Bailey the confidence she'd have felt in a big-city, multi-partner women's clinic.

She'd already had Bailey's records faxed to her from her doctor in Manhattan. But what made Bailey the most comfortable was that the doctor, too, was pregnant. And at about the same stage.

"Seven months along yourself, Dr. Lee?" Bailey asked her.

She nodded. "Give or take a week. Please call me Elizabeth. I'm due January 8, but I'm impatient about everything. And I haven't bought Christmas gifts yet. I may just make everyone a grandmother, an aunt, a godmother for Christmas."

She weighed Bailey and did all the usual tests, though the little hospital's equipment didn't run to an ultrasound.

Bailey told her about her late-night distress and Jeff's back rub.

She smiled from Bailey to Jeff. "That's the best thing you can do. With a father on the 'outside,' so to speak, he should take advantage of his chances for contact. I think men who give good back rubs should get bonuses, like a night out with the boys every week, or a week-long hunting trip."

Then Elizabeth sat down opposite Bailey and Jeff and pointed her pen at Bailey.

"We have to plump you up a little bit," she said, looking over her notes. "You're on Phenergan, so I assume you've had a rough time. Is it working for you?"

Bailey nodded. "Every once in a while I forget to take it."

Elizabeth pointed her pen at Jeff. "That's something else you can do for her. Forgetfulness is a little bit of a problem in the third trimester, so while you're giving her those back rubs, you might check to make sure she's taken her meds and gotten her exercise." She turned to Bailey. "You are getting some?"

"Well..." Bailey winced guiltily. "Except for running for the subway or a taxi, no. Working took most of my time. We...I...just got here yesterday."

She nodded. "So Mr. McIntyre explained. Your records say you're single?" She smiled from Bailey to Jeff. "I'm not prying, but support at home is important for a pregnant woman. Are you a nine-to-five back rubber?"

Jeff grinned. "No, I live in. It's my baby, Doctor Bailey's staying with me."

"All right, then. You're looking good, Bailey. I'd say try to eat a little more, get in some moderate exercise. Walking's good. When you're intimate, condoms are a good idea at this stage to prevent infection." She handed Bailey a printed sheet. "This is a good basic diet. You are eating for two, and though you don't have to have twice the calories, every calorie you ingest should count nutritionally. And don't forget to drink your milk and a lot of water. Okay." She put her notes on her lap and crossed her hands over them. "Any concerns or questions I can answer?"

Bailey shook her head, but Jeff spoke up. "I have one," he said. "She's small. Is this going to be a problem for her when she delivers?"

Elizabeth shook her head. "No. Sometimes a large woman can have a smaller pelvis, and a small woman can have a roomy one. Bailey's average. She should be fine. I'm offering Lamaze classes right here Thursday nights at 7:30 if you'd like to join us. There's nothing quite as comforting as being prepared."

Jeff shook her hand. "We'll be here."

The doctor smiled at Bailey when Jeff didn't even consult her. "Unfortunately it's a fact of nature that the same hands that can give a good back rub often take charge of a situation without asking anyone else. Does the class sound like a good idea to you?"

There was no point in argument for argument's sake. Taking Lamaze classes was the sensible thing to do. But she was grateful to her for asking. "Yes, it does." Then, because she noticed Elizabeth wasn't wearing a ring, she asked, "Do you have someone for back rubs?"

Elizabeth looked momentarily startled, then distressed, then her smiling self again. "Actually, I don't. But I'm on the lookout for one. Tell your friends."

"We have to find her somebody," Bailey said to Jeff as they walked down the path to the car.

"She was kidding about the 'tell your friends' remark, Bailey." He opened her door and helped her into the passenger seat. "People don't always appreciate matchmaking efforts. Especially if it doesn't work out."

She frowned at him as he climbed in behind the wheel. "I thought you were all for love and commitment."

"I am," he agreed, putting the key in the ignition. "Ours. I wouldn't presume to arrange it for someone else."

Ours. She repeated the word to herself. Ours. His and hers. It had a nice round sound that made her want to think about something else before she got too comfortable with it.

"What now?" she asked.

"Slippers have slipped to priority number three," he said, letting a green van pass before turning into the light midmorning traffic. "Fattening you up is priority two. How about a latte at the bakery? Decaf, of course. You can get your calories and some milk, too." He smiled blandly. "And I can get an apple fritter and an Americano."

"What's an Americano?"

"Strong black coffee."

"So your attention-getting charm has an ulterior motive. She said my calories had to count nutritionally."

"You can get a bagel or a scone."

She capitulated. "Okay, I'm sold."

The latte was delicious, and after she raved over the scone, Jeff bought several to take home. Then he bought her fleece-lined slipper boots for general wear and woolly scuffs to keep by the bed for middle-of-the-night excursions to the bathroom or the kitchen.

They bought groceries before going home.

As they walked into The Way Station, three men in gray coveralls rose from the sofa in the lobby at a signal from Maureen. Sonny, just returning with an empty room-service tray, set it aside behind the desk and came to take the groceries from Jeff.

"I'll carry them up for you, Mr. McIntyre," he offered.

"Thanks, Sonny."

"Jeff, these gentlemen are from Up and Down Situation. They said you asked them to come by today..." Her impeccably professional expression became a questioning grimace. "About installing an elevator?"

A man who appeared to be in his late forties or early fifties stepped forward and offered his hand. "Buddy Marsh, Mr. McIntyre. My boys, Tom and Paul. We've walked around the property," he said, "and looked around inside. For convenience from your suite, I'd say we put it back here, in the northwest corner."

He started to walk in that direction. Jeff raised a finger to halt him, then called to Sonny, who'd just started up the stairs. Sonny came back. "Yes, sir?"

"Would you take Bailey upstairs, please?" To Bailey, he said, "I'll be a little while. Why don't you call room service for lunch? Thank you, Maureen."

Bailey allowed herself to be escorted upstairs, thanked Sonny for his help, then put the groceries away. Then she got her bags of fabric, spread their contents all over the dining table while thinking about the men in the lobby.

She smiled over the name of their business. Up and Down Situation. What a great name for a company that built elevators.

She remembered from the last time she'd been at The Way Station when Maureen had told her that all previous owners of the hotel had resisted adding an elevator in order to maintain the integrity of the original architecture. He was breaking with tradition— and probably alienating the historical society—because of her. For two months' duration, it hardly seemed necessary.

She would have protested, then remembered Sonny's struggles up and down the stairs and decided to be quiet.

She put thoughts of Jeff out of her mind in order to concentrate on cutting and piecing the green fabrics, then noticed with a smile in the middle of the process how much more at peace she was when she *didn't* think of him. Because there were all those aggravating assumptions of control to compare with those thoughtful things he did—but that was thinking about him. She turned her mind off again and focused on the quilt.

JEFF HEADED BACK to his office with his copy of the contract he'd just signed with Up and Down Situation. They'd promised him the standard-size car built within a filigreed iron cage so it looked like something from the turn of the century. He was pleased.

He pushed his office door open and was surprised to find the room occupied by Matt and Justin. Josie must have said something to them.

Matt sat in the chair at Jeff's desk and Justin sat in the chair beside it. Matt looked interested. Justin seemed amused. Their Stetsons were on Jeff's hat rack.

Jeff walked into the office and closed the door. "Let me guess," he said, tossing the contract over Justin's head and onto the desk. "You're here on a fact-finding mission."

"I'm wounded," Matt said with a theatrical hand to his heart. He turned to Justin. "Are you wounded?"

"Deeply," Justin replied.

Justin rose and pushed Jeff into his chair. Matt rolled back from the desk so that he could look Jeff in the eye.

"You misjudge us." Matt's tone was a little sanctimonious and belied by the humor in his eyes. "The truth is, we heard the news from Josie yesterday and thought you might need a little support. When you weren't at Rotary today, we thought we'd stop by and see if you were all right.'' He looked him over in concern. ''Are you?''

''I'm fine,'' Jeff replied, leaning back in his chair and angling one leg over the other knee. ''A little surprised…temporarily, you know, off balance. But fine.''

Matt slapped him on the shoulder. ''At least you're not alone. Puts you in the same position as Justin. You'll get each other through.''

Justin nodded. ''It'll take some adjustment. Once the baby comes, your life's no longer your own. Your *wife's* no longer your own. She'll be a slave to this baby pretty much all the time.'' He levelled his gaze on Jeff. ''But Bailey's not your wife. That's got to be a problem for you that I'm not facing.''

Matt picked up on that. ''You're going to invest a lot of effort and emotion into the next two months. What are you going to do if…she doesn't stay?''

''She'll stay,'' Jeff said. He always thought of his intentions as fact. Jeff was having difficulty talking to Matt about this subject, given that an accident had taken away Matt's wife and unborn child.

''But what if she doesn't?''

Jeff stared Matt down. ''It doesn't matter. I gave her a baby. I owe her the next few months.''

''Well, don't be too self-sacrificing. I think she owes you a little, too. You should get a lawyer if you're going to want to share custody.''

''He threatened to fight for full custody,'' Justin put in. ''My man! That's how he got her here.''

Matt frowned. ''You mean, you're going to have to *fight* to share this baby?''

Jeff shook his head. "No." There were times when a caring family was more of a hindrance than a help. "It took intimidation to get her here, but keeping the baby to herself wasn't any kind of revenge on her part, just...a need for independence."

"Independence," Justin repeated. "That doesn't sound promising."

"Do you love her?" Matt asked. He had a knack for getting to the heart of an issue. "Or are you just trying to do the right thing?"

"Either way," Jeff replied, "it comes out the same."

Matt shook his head. "You know it doesn't. If you love her, you can get hurt."

"And how do I defend myself against that? Decide *not* to love her?"

"So you do?"

"Hell, I don't know." Jeff sank into the chair in exasperation. "I did when I made love to her, then she walked away in search of her freedom and I thought I'd forgotten her. So I bump into her in New York all swollen with my baby and my first instinct is to shake her and yell at her, but under it all I'm really glad to see her. And glad to have the baby to use as a lever to make her come back with me." He ran a hand slowly down his face. "Yeah. I love her."

"Does she know that?" Justin asked.

Jeff shook his head. "We've agreed to just coexist until the baby comes."

Matt stared at him grimly for a moment, then turned to Jeff. "That doesn't leave this room. He's going to have enough trouble dealing with her without Josie telling her how he feels."

Justin nodded agreement.

"You're bringing her to dinner on Sunday?" Matt stood and pushed his chair in.

Jeff could just imagine what an ordeal that was going to be for Bailey and for himself, with his brother and Justin assessing her suitability and Josie watching him for signs of love.

And then, of course, there would be Willie, who always watched everyone for reasons of her own.

"Sure." He got to his feet as Matt and Justin went to the door.

"Josie's going to expect you to have a brilliant idea for advertising the baby contest," Justin warned. At Jeff's despondent look he added, both hands raised in innocence, "I just thought you'd like to know. You wouldn't want to be unprepared for her attack, would you?"

"God, no." Jeff walked Matt and Justin across the lobby to the door. "See you guys on Sunday."

Justin went outside but Matt lingered just inside the doors. "You might also be prepared for a call from Mom." He patted Jeff's arm consolingly. "She's racking up the potential grandchildren and is really affronted by the thought that she came close to missing one. You might warn Bailey, too."

Jeff put an arm around Matt's shoulders and walked him out. As a kid, he'd been a despotic older brother, but as an adult, he'd been the best friend Jeff and Alex could have asked for. It still hurt Jeff to know that two years ago, in Matt's darkest hour, there'd been nothing he'd been able to do for him.

Chapter Six

"Hello?" Bailey answered the phone, a length of fabric over her shoulder, a pair of scissors in her hand. Then, realizing a strange voice answering Jeff's phone might be confusing to the caller, she added quickly, "Jeff McIntyre's residence."

There was a brief hesitation, then an imperious female voice asked, "Bailey Dutton?"

Bailey felt a ripple of dread along her spine. She was certain the voice belonged to Debra McIntyre, Jeff's mother. She squared her shoulders, berated herself for being a coward and replied in a polite but firm tone, "Yes. Hello, Mrs. McIntyre. How are you?"

"Well, I think I'm fine," she replied, "But I'd be more sure if I knew you weren't going to abscond with one of my grandchildren the moment it's born." Bailey heard a low voice in the background, then Debra shushing it. A small struggle seemed to ensue, then a male voice came on the line.

"Bailey?" It was Ken McIntyre, Jeff's father. "How are you? Josie said you've been pretty ill."

Bailey felt herself relax just a little. She'd danced

with him at Josie's wedding, and he'd been funny and kind.

"Hi, Mr. McIntyre. I'm fine. I was sick, but medication takes care of the problem...as long as I remember to take it. How's your golf game? You told me at the wedding you were so desperate to improve, you were going to take lessons."

He laughed. "I'm taking lessons, all right, but so far I'm still desperate." There was more kibitzing in the background, this time from Debra, and Ken cleared his throat.

Bailey braced herself, sure he was being coached to get down to business.

"We're...so glad you and Jeff ran into each other," he said. Bailey was sure that was the diplomatic version of whatever it was Debra wanted him to say. "I'm also glad you came home with him. Your baby should be born among his family."

"And he should *stay* there," she heard Debra add.

Bailey swallowed and cleared her own throat. "The baby's a 'she,'" she corrected. "Josie's been very welcoming and Jeff..." As she said his name, she looked up to see him standing there, his jacket hooked over his shoulder by his index finger. He frowned at her questioningly.

She turned her attention back to the conversation. "Jeff's made me very comfortable," she went on, "but as I'm always reminding him, the baby is only *half* McIntyre."

There was silence on the other end of the line. Oh, God. Now she'd done it.

"You can assure Mrs. McIntyre that Jeff and I are going to share—" She stopped abruptly when Jeff took the phone from her. He dropped his jacket on the back of a chair and walked restlessly into the kitchen.

Bailey followed him, now worried about what he intended to say.

"Dad, hi. It's Jeff. Yeah, I'm good. How are you? All right. How's Mom? Oh, hi, Mom. Good, I'm glad you're both on. Yeah, I'm sorry I haven't called yet. I wasn't deliberately keeping you in the dark, I've just been getting Bailey settled in...."

Bailey stood by anxiously as Jeff exchanged more small talk with his parents, then she heard his mother's voice on the other end of the line, a little high, slightly agitated.

"Don't worry about it," Jeff replied, leaning back against the counter. "We can handle it, whatever happens.... No, Mom, I know what you think without being told."

Bailey crossed her hands in front of him in an emphatic negative, not wanting him to say anything to upset his parents. No, she mouthed. Don't—

He stopped her by catching her hands in his free one. "No. I'll keep you posted, just trust us to make the right decision. You raised me, remember? And please don't pressure Bailey about the baby. She's got enough to worry about right now."

Bailey shook her head at him. He ignored her.

"That's not what I meant, Mom. You're welcome to call anytime. In fact, I'm sure Bailey would love to hear from you with encouragement or support." He listened, then added, "Good. I'm glad you weren't. I wouldn't like it if you did."

Bailey dropped her head with a groan, certain

she'd been responsible for the destruction of the McIntyre family—or Jeff's relationship within it, anyway.

Jeff listened. "Sure," he said finally. "It'd be great to have you home for Christmas. Lucky for you all the grandchildren are due at the same time, so you can probably cover all the births in one visit.... What would Matt have going on? He's there by himself.... Well, if he does start renting out rooms and there's no place for you, there's always room here.... Sure. I love you, too.... No, she's right here. You want to say goodbye?"

Jeff handed Bailey the phone and left the room.

His mother apologized. "I didn't mean to sound as though I was picking on you," she said in a warmer voice. "Our children are still everything to us, even though they're adults. We want them to be happy. And I just...don't know how he can be happy without his child. Ken, I'm just being honest," she said in an aside to her husband. "She was honest with me. I'm sure she appreciates it."

"I do, Mrs. McIntyre," Bailey said, relaxing a little as the woman seemed to relax. Maybe she hadn't destroyed the family after all. "I promise you I'm not out to hurt Jeff. And whatever decision we make, we'll make together."

"That's fair enough," Ken McIntyre said. "Isn't it, Deb?"

"Yes," Debra conceded with a sigh. Bailey wasn't entirely sure she believed her. "It's fair enough."

They said their goodbyes and Bailey pressed the off button on the phone. She put it down on the table and went in search of Jeff. She found him standing near his bed. He'd changed into faded jeans and was pulling a Bison City Bugle Centennial sweatshirt over his head.

He emerged from the neck, his blue eyes bright against the gray, his rumpled hair lending a seductive quality to his usually pulled-together appearance. He ran his fingers through the thick dark stuff to restore it to order.

She stood in the middle of the doorway, hands behind her back, trying to deal with her gratitude. He could have used his parents' call to his advantage, but he hadn't. He'd come to her defense.

"Thank you for that," she said as he pushed a dresser drawer closed, then came toward her. "I hope your parents aren't angry at you."

"They're not angry at anybody," he said. "They just care a lot and sometimes that makes them nosier than they should be. What did you have for lunch?"

She stopped to think. She'd intended to have lunch. She'd put the groceries away, pulled out her fabric to measure and plan....

Jeff shook his head at her, turned her toward the kitchen and gently pushed her there. "Bailey, how can you forget to eat? Didn't you hear anything Elizabeth said? It's important for you and the baby that you eat well."

"I didn't deliberately *not* eat," she said as he went to the meatkeeper. "For a long time, eating wasn't a pleasurable experience, but today you made breakfast, you got me a latte and a bagel when we left the doctor's office. I think I just didn't get hungry."

He put a butcher's foam tray of chicken breasts on the counter and gave her a teasing look over the top of the refrigerator door as he pointed to the dining table still strewn with material. "I think it's the fabric. Makes you forget to come home, so it probably also made you forget to eat."

"It's for a quilt for Josie's baby," she said defensively.

"That's nice. What about our baby?"

She looked a little sheepish. "I have a whole bunch of pink stuff for that."

He smiled. "All right. Broccoli or asparagus?"

"Depends. Can you make Hollandaise sauce for the asparagus?" she asked with a straight face.

"Aren't we clever?" He handed her a fat stalk of broccoli. "Put that in the steamer. In that cupboard to the left of the sink, in the pull-out drawer. Potatoes or rice?"

"Rice, please."

Bailey completed her assigned task, then went to move her fabric off the dining table.

"You can leave it there." He looked up from putting a lid on a pot of rice. "There's no place else to stretch out a project like that. We'll eat on the sofa." He looked doubtful for a moment. "Or can you, with Noelle in the way?"

She tapped the top of her mounded stomach. "I've discovered that I can put my plate right here on her feet."

"Good. Coffee, tea, cocoa, milk?"

She smiled in surprise. "You have cocoa?"

"Yeah. It's instant, though."

She wandered idly toward him, thinking that he was even more interesting than she'd originally thought all those months ago when she'd fallen for his charm and his competence. "Instant's great. I love cocoa. But I'm surprised you have it around. I guess I figured you for a bourbon and branchwater kind of man."

He laughed. "I have a sudden picture of myself at a card table on a riverboat. I'm wearing a panama hat, smoking a cheroot and beating suckers out of their gold."

She winced. "Wrong part of the country? What do cowboys in Wyoming drink?"

"Whisky or beer, I guess. But I have a preference for scotch and water. And cocoa. But not together. Can you reach the cups?"

Within half an hour they were seated side by side on the sofa, watching the evening news while eating dinner. Bailey was struck by the comfortable domesticity of it.

Replete with the simple but delicious meal, she tried to sit up to clear away the dishes, but fell back again into the deep, soft sofa

"I forgot about this sofa," she groaned, trying again. "I think it's going to require heavy equipment to get me up."

Jeff rose gracefully. "Just relax. I'll get dessert." Then he noticed her feet, still in her tennies. "Where'd you put your slippers?"

"They're still in the bag on my bed."

He disappeared toward the bedrooms, then returned, pulling the tags off the woolly slipper-boots. He removed her shoes and put the slippers on her.

She wriggled her toes inside them. "They feel wonderful."

"That's the idea."

He brought her some raspberry frozen yogurt in a coffee mug and a second cup of cocoa.

She accepted them guiltily. "I'll cook the rest of the week. I'm not gourmet quality, but fairly competent."

"Don't worry about it. Whoever's available can do it. Meanwhile relax and enjoy that. We're getting you out for a walk after a while."

She stopped with a spoon of yogurt halfway to her mouth. "It's dark."

He grinned. "You can be out in the dark if you're with me. When we get our schedule better organized, we can walk mornings or afternoons, if you'd prefer. But we've got to start building you up."

She took the bite of yogurt. "You sound as though you're preparing me for the pregnant women's wrestling circuit. I'll be fine."

He looked doubtful as he sat down beside her. She remembered his concern in the doctor's office over her ability to deliver because of her small body structure. She'd been both touched and amused, and tried not to think too hard about it. Added to all his other kindnesses today, it was insidiously endearing.

THE NEWS HOUR OVER, Jeff was about to lean forward to reach the remote when Bailey's head slid against his shoulder. She was asleep, her empty cocoa cup still hooked in her fingers. So much for her walk.

He gently disengaged the cup, then reached an arm out to put it on the coffee table without moving the rest of his body. He turned toward her, eased her head off his arm and onto his chest, then caught the dark blue crocheted afghan on the back of the sofa and covered her with it. It had been a gift from Matt's wife, Julie.

Bailey lifted her head and half opened her eyes. "Can we walk...later?" she asked.

"Sure." He pulled her head back to his chest and readjusted the blanket on her shoulders. "Go back to sleep."

He realized with a smile that he needn't have bothered with the advice. She was out like a light. He guessed she was still recovering from their middle-of-the-night flight.

He channel surfed, found an old World War II movie and watched it in its entirety. Bailey never stirred, except to wrap her arm around his waist. Noelle moved more than she did. He felt her fairly regular kicks against his abdomen and put a hand to her, amazed anew that he was making contact with his daughter across the fragile boundary of Bailey's body, the curtain between prelife and life.

The circle they made at that moment was life the way he'd wanted it since he'd returned to Bison City. It was family. He made himself remember that this was just a momentary thing. He and Bailey were getting along, but in spite of all his big talk in front of his brother and Justin that afternoon, he had no idea if he could make her stay. Her need for freedom was a living, breathing thing inside her—right beside their baby.

If she gave birth to both of them, he was sunk.

He considered that for a full minute, just to make sure he gave himself a good dose of reality, then dismissed it altogether in acceptance of the also-real truth that a McIntyre was never sunk. He may flounder, swallow water, go under twice, but he was never sunk.

Somehow he was going to convince Bailey to stay.

Just before eleven he lifted her in his arms and carried her into her room. He put her in the middle of the bed, pulled off her slippers and wondered what to do about the dress she wore.

As though trying to cooperate, she turned drowsily onto her side, allowing him access to the zipper. He pulled it down, tipped her gently onto her back again and pulled the arms of the dress off her. The rest of it slid off easily. He removed her slip and allowed himself a moment to feast his eyes on her full breasts in white lace, and her large belly in simple white cotton. She looked like a very beautiful fertility sculpture.

Deciding that going any farther might frighten her if she woke up, he looked for that cotton nightgown she wore and found it sticking out from under her pillow.

Getting her head through the neck hole and her arms into the sleeves was easy, but he had to sit beside her and lift her upper body into his arms to smooth it down her back and tie two small flat buttons that had not been made for a man's hands.

"Jeff," she murmured sleepily.

"Yes?" he asked.

"Is it time to walk?" She yawned, but she continued to lean heavily on him while he worked.

"No. Too late. We'll walk tomorrow." The buttons finally buttoned, he put her back against the pillows and had to pry her arms from around his neck.

"Sleepy," she said, turning onto her side again. "'Night."

He took advantage of the moment to draw the skirt of the nightgown down, then pulled the blankets up over her.

He felt as though he'd just conquered Everest without a guide. His hands were trembling with the need to touch, to hold, to own.

But she wanted freedom, and he was beginning to realize that the only way to convince her that it wasn't really what she wanted was to let her have it.

So he turned out her light and went back into the living room to lock up for the night.

HE AWOKE TO THE SMELL of peanut butter. It was 4:02 a.m. The smell of peanut butter, he thought he remembered, signaled the onset of a stroke. No. That was burned toast.

He heard small sounds from the kitchen and realized that the smell of peanut butter probably signaled the awakening of someone who'd fallen asleep at seven-thirty the night before.

God…4:02 a.m. What had happened to his simple life?

He got up in the shorts and T-shirt he always wore to bed and went to check on her.

There were cookies everywhere except the dining table, which was still covered with her fabric. They were spread on foil and cooling on the coffee table, on the counters, on the chopping-block top of the dishwasher. Over her nightgown, Bailey wore the blue-and-white-striped Cordon Bleu apron she must have found in a drawer. It was hooked around her neck but untied. In her condition the strings weren't long enough. She had an oven mitt on one hand and a spatula in the other and walked back and forth in front of the oven, apparently waiting for a pan of cookies to finish.

She looked like an eccentric field marshal.

When the timer rang, she opened the oven, took one pan out and placed it on the cold burners of the stove—the only uncovered surface in the kitchen—then put another pan in and reset the timer.

He leaned against the edge of the counter. "Mrs. Fields, I assume?" he asked.

She turned in surprise, spatula raised as though in defense. Then she used it to scoop up a cooling cookie and offer it to him. "Hi," she said. "I suppose I woke you. I'm sorry. I don't remember going to bed, but I woke up at about two-thirty feeling very rested."

She did look bright and fresh.

He nodded and took the cookie. "You dozed off right after dinner. I finally put you to bed around eleven. What's with the cookies?"

He took a bite and quickly decided she didn't have to have a reason for them. It was rich and buttery with the snap a good cookie should have. He'd never appreciated the gourmet trend of soft-baked cookies.

A faint shadow crossed her eyes. "Josie called this afternoon and said your family always has Sunday dinner together."

"Right."

"And I'd be expected."

"Yes."

She gestured with her padded hand. "I thought I'd

take cookies. I know today's only Saturday, but they
should have a day to crisp up in tins." Then she
looked around at the sea of fork-flattened peanut butter discs and asked in mild concern, "Do we have
tins?"

He shrugged a shoulder. "We'll buy some." He
popped the last bite of cookie into his mouth and
helped himself to another. "I didn't know you had
domestic tendencies."

She pinched the mitt between her arm and her side
and pulled her hand out. "Just a few small ones."
She winced and rubbed the small of her back. Then
she asked worriedly, "Your brothers are going to
hate me, aren't they?"

He put the cookie down and pulled her into his
arms so he could rub her back. "No, they won't. You
upset about Mom's call?"

BAILEY HELD ON TO HIM for balance as he worked
on her back. He had such a sure and comforting
touch.

"Not upset," she answered. "When I first decided
to keep the baby to myself, the only people I considered were you and me. And I guess because all
my family's gone, I sort of forgot that your family's
so close and that Noelle has aunts and uncles and
grandparents to think about."

"That's true." He massaged slow circles precisely
where she always felt the weight of her pregnancy
when she'd spent too much time on her feet. "But
in the end, it's your life. I just want to make sure the
baby will be part of mine. But we should be able to
do that without destroying your plans for the future.

It's not ideal, but nothing ever is. How many more pans to go?''

''Ah...'' For a minute she couldn't process the question. He was being so reasonable, she was caught off guard. From the moment he'd walked into the advertising firm's photo studio, he'd wanted to take control of a situation about which he was clearly, understandably angry.

She'd cooperated to a degree because she knew she'd been wrong not to tell him about Noelle and because she didn't doubt for a minute that he'd take her to court.

Maybe a couple of days at home had mellowed him. The security of his home turf was allowing him to make some concessions.

That was good. It set her just a little off balance, but that was because she hadn't expected him to understand her need to be free of binding relationships.

''This is the...last pan.'' She straightened up and took a step backward. ''Thanks. That helped a lot. I'll get everything cleaned up, don't worry. And I'll fix breakfast.''

He picked up the rest of his cookie. ''I was thinking we'd walk to the Silver Horn Grill on the interstate. It's just about a half mile away, and we can get exercise and breakfast at the same time. You have comfortable shoes?''

''My tennies are comfortable.''

''How's seven o'clock?''

''Perfect.''

''All right.'' He gave her a perfunctory kiss on the forehead. ''I'm going back to bed.''

Bailey watched his long, strong legs beneath the

dark blue boxers walk away from her, his broad back nicely defined in the white T-shirt, and felt inexplicably dissatisfied.

Then the timer dinged and she pulled her glove back on and went to the stove.

THE TWO MCINTYRE BROTHERS, Bailey thought, along with Josie's husband, looked like a lineup of soap opera hunks or Hollywood heartthrobs. In height and weight, Matt and Jeff looked as though they'd been cloned. They both had dark hair and blue eyes, but with a subtle difference in the shade. The strong, square features were similar, though stamped with the defining qualities of their characters as Josie had described them to her—Matt's steadiness, Jeff's gift for insight and determination. The absent Alex was purported to be wild.

Justin, with light brown hair and gray eyes, had a similar body type. He seemed very much his own person, but was clearly accepted as one of them, judging by the amount of friendly abuse he took.

Bailey felt like an outsider. Not that a woman could ever penetrate the circle that seemed to close around the men when they were in the same room. And not that they hadn't welcomed her warmly enough, but she sensed a certain reserve in their treatment of her.

Willie, Matt's housekeeper, was coolly polite as she relieved her of the stack of tins. Even that courtesy, Bailey guessed, was a hardship for her.

"She thinks she's our surrogate mother," Josie said under her breath as she whipped something yellow and frothy in a pottery bowl.

Willie handed Bailey a large, golden onion and pointed her to a chopping block and a knife waiting on the end of the counter.

"Oh-oh," Josie teased, turning off the mixer. "Did you do something wrong already? You just got here."

Bailey smiled. "No. It's just that my onion-chopping skills are known worldwide. Willie's probably heard of me."

Willie looked her over with a little frown, apparently confused by her insistent good humor. "I'd like the onion in wedges, please."

"Right." Bailey chopped the ends off and began to peel.

"How do you like Bison City?" Josie asked as she poured the contents of her bowl into a cake pan. "I've lived here all my life, but you must be suffering severe culture shock after working in New York City."

"I've found a lot to like about it," Bailey replied, ignoring her stinging eyes. "The bakery, the Silver Horn Grill and The Way Station—they're wonderful places."

Josie put the cake pan in the oven, then moved to the middle of the counter where a collection of salad makings waited in a colander. She began to pull apart a head of romaine. "I could be happy living at the hotel. I'd never leave that big chair by the fireplace in the lobby."

Bailey laughed. "I can never leave the sofa in Jeff's suite. Once I sit down, it's impossible to get up without a crane."

"Yeah, that is becoming a problem." Josie blotted

leaves of romaine on a lineup of paper towels. "I've already graduated to slip-on shoes and sleeping sitting up. I half expect to open my mouth to brush my teeth and find baby toes sticking out of it."

Bailey burst into laughter at the image.

Jeff walked into the kitchen, looked around and, spotting the tins on the small table, went to retrieve the top one. He stood with it in one hand and pretended displeasure at their hilarity

"And how do you intend to put dinner on the table when you're wasting time laughing?"

Willie shook her head at him, a slight twitch of her lips contradicting a frown. "They're the worst kitchen crew a body ever had."

"Where are you going with that?" Josie asked, pointing a spoon at the tin he carried. "What's in there, anyway?"

"Bailey's peanut butter cookies," he replied. "And if you weren't fooling around, you could probably have one. But I can see you'll have to keep your nose to the grind—"

Before he could finish, Josie had ripped the tin from his grasp, opened it and passed it around. Bailey was a little surprised to see Willie take one.

"Well." Jeff looked chagrined. "It hurts to see how little the comfort of your menfolk means to you."

Josie turned to him to give him a full view of her eighth-month tummy. "And look at what all of you have done to us. I don't think our comfort is on your minds, either." She placed the tin on the counter beside her. "These will only spoil your dinner," she pronounced.

"Well, where *are* these cookies you've been bragging about?" Justin appeared in the kitchen doorway. "I thought you were coming right back with them."

Jeff went to the table to commandeer another tin. "I'd intended to, but I ran into a little trouble with the scullery maids."

Justin came to take it from him. "We don't want excuses, pal. Just results." He walked back into the living room, the tin tucked under his arm.

Jeff spread his arms in pained indignation. "Cookies made with my ingredients, in my kitchen, and I don't even get to taste one."

Josie shook her head at her companions, who dutifully lamented his whining, then offered him the tin. "Here. Have one of ours."

"They're not yours, they're *mine*," he insisted, reaching for one.

Matt walked up behind him and snatched the cookie from his hand. "They're in my house. I think that makes them mine." He bit into it as he headed for the back door. He stopped, his hand on the knob, and chewed and swallowed. He raised an eyebrow at Bailey. "These are perfect. Crisp. I haven't had really good peanut butter cookies since..." He hesitated only briefly, then covered the pause with a smile for Bailey. "My wife was a good baker. This family could use you. Josie burns everything, and Willie's too busy."

Willie gave him a look of righteous indignation. "And I suppose I *never* bake you anything? What about the coffee bread last Sunday morning? The apple pie on Tuesday? The butterflake rolls every Friday of your life because you like them with my stew?''

He nodded. ''You're a treasure, Willie. But you never make cookies,'' he said over his shoulder as he went out the back door.

''You never asked for cookies!''

''If I don't get a cookie right now,'' Jeff threatened, ''no one's hearing my brilliant idea for an ad campaign for the baby contest.''

Matt walked through with an armload of wood. ''Are you still whining?'' he asked.

Josie handed Jeff the tin. ''Okay, what is it?''

''I'll tell you after dinner,'' he said, and walked away with the cookies.

Josie shook her head after him. ''What can I say? Growing up between Matt and Alex, how could he be expected to turn out sane?''

The teasing, Bailey observed, was ruthless and constant and interspersed with more serious exchanges and family news. Dinner was delicious and long. Matt invited Willie to join them, but she insisted she wasn't hungry and had to put some finishing touches on dessert.

They dawdled over coffee, and the men even had more cookies after dessert.

Bailey grew a little uncomfortable, trying unobtrusively to stretch her torso against the ever pervasive lower-back pain.

Jeff, though talking across the table to Matt, noticed and began to rub it for her without missing a beat in the conversation.

Josie smiled commiseratingly as she stacked dishes. ''I haven't had to deal with that yet, thank goodness. But you're carrying so low. No, don't get up. I'll carry these in.''

Justin watched her walk into the kitchen with a fond smile. ''I swear that woman's carrying an engine. Pregnancy seems to have revved her up rather than slowed her down. A revved-up Josie is sort of like Fran Fine on fast-forward.''

''I heard that!'' Josie shouted from the kitchen.

Chapter Seven

"Okay, Mr. Advertising's Man of the Year," Josie said as she placed a fresh pot of coffee in the middle of the table. "Let's hear your ideas. Or should I even be speaking in the plural?"

Willie placed a tray with a bottle of brandy and glasses beside the coffeepot, then pushed on Josie's shoulder until she sat down. "You shouldn't be speaking at all," she said. "You should be listening."

Justin patted Josie's knee. "Do you know how that's done, sweetheart? You..."

She pointed a threatening finger at him while fighting a grin. Her brothers laughed heartily.

"Thanks, Willie." Jeff accepted a cup of coffee from the housekeeper, and when the laughter finally died down, he focused on his sister. "Okay, listen up. I'm not sure this qualifies as brilliant, but I think it'll work."

The women leaned toward him around the table, and the men sat back, sipping at their coffee and waiting. "I think your big edge here is that the news has been full of millennium doom and gloom—the weather's changing, cosmic disasters are predicted, the computer trauma Y2K thing—all that stuff. But what's happening here in Bison City?''

"Babies," Josie and Bailey replied simultaneously.

"Exactly. The dictionary describes the millennium as a period of great happiness and human perfection. So, right here in Bison City, we're giving birth to— the Millennium Baby. I think that's what you should call your contest. Who wouldn't want to enroll their baby for a chance at the title of the perfect baby? And, of course, there are all those prizes." He frowned and leaned toward Josie. "The only thing that bothers me about it is that your money-making ability is limited to pregnant women."

"But it's a baby contest," Josie said. "It pretty much has to be, doesn't it?"

Willie spoke up. "You could have other money-making things that surround it. You know, bake sales, crafts and things that we could sell at the Thanksgiving Fair."

Bailey frowned. "We need something like that to focus our efforts in one place, so people would really want to buy or take a chance because it's related to the babies. What could that be?"

Josie rested her chin in her hand. "You mean something that would connect whoever makes a purchase or a donation to the babies?"

"Or the winning baby," Jeff said.

They stared at each other. Then Justin asked, "What about if we had a raffle to have your photo taken with the Millennium Baby? The *Bison City Bugle* would run it on the front page, and as a human interest story, it might be picked up by other, bigger papers. People would pay a dollar for that, wouldn't they? You know, we could bill it as 'Hold the baby who holds all the promise of the new millennium.' Something like that.''

Josie leaned toward him to kiss his cheek. "That's brilliant, Justin.''

Jeff narrowed his gaze in thought. It was the bud of a good idea, but not quite full-blown. Just as he was trying to see through it to its potential to become what they needed, Bailey raised both arms in the air with an excited exclamation. "I've got it!''

Her left arm collided with his right one and sloshed half the contents of his cup onto the table-cloth.

"Oh, geez!" Everyone pushed napkins her way to sop it up. "I'm sorry.''

Willie appeared with a tea towel to put under the cloth to protect the wood. "Must be quite an idea,'' she observed.

Jeff sent Willie a scolding look and put a comforting hand to Bailey's back. "It's all right,'' he said. "This is a messy group. That happens at least once every Sunday.'' She was having a somewhat trying afternoon, he knew, thanks to Willie, but was behaving with remarkable good humor.

When they'd first arrived, Matt and Justin had been impeccably polite but kept her at a careful distance, waiting for her to redeem herself for having kept a McIntyre from them. But she'd won them over with wit and courtesy—and her cookies hadn't hurt.

Willie was the only holdout, taking every opportunity to offer a subtle zing or gibe. Bailey had met them all with a persistent smile.

"So, what's the idea?" he asked.

"It's just a refinement of everything else that's come up," she said, smiling across the table at Josie's husband. "It came together when Justin mentioned photographing the winner of the raffle. What if we create a Millennium Baby calendar, then there'd be twelve winners. Twelve people could have their photos taken with the first baby born on January first. They sign up for a dollar to be included, then not only does the hospital get those donations, but we can then sell the calendar. Of course, every one of the twelve winners would get a free one."

There was a moment's silence then Josie screamed. "That's it! Bailey, that's it!" She turned to Justin. "Don't you think?"

He nodded enthusiastically. "Works for me. It makes money from all kinds of angles, has the potential to draw more people in because it's different and appealing, and—with the *Bugle* being able to print tickets, calendars, whatever—it won't cost much more than supplies."

"Bailey can design the calendar," Jeff volunteered for her, "and I can do the copy, develop the ads and whatever else we need."

Justin pushed away from the table. "I guess this means a news article about this meeting. Be right back. Camera's in the car."

They talked until early evening refining ideas and helping Justin develop a news story. He took a few photos of Josie and Bailey at work at the table.

"I'll run the story inside the TV section insert, so subscribers can look at it all week."

Josie was beside herself with excitement. Jeff and Bailey earned hearty hugs. "We could take over the world with this collection of brain power," she said.

Justin laughed. "Let's work on organizing our lives first. And getting this pediatric wing built."

Matt walked everyone out to their cars. Hugs and handshakes were exchanged again, and Jeff noticed that Matt hugged Bailey, then passed her on to Justin, who wrapped her in his arms.

"I'm trusting you to be a good influence on Josie," Justin said. "Her latest escapade was a Chinese fire drill on Maine and Aspen at 5:00 p.m."

"I thought one of the tires felt funny and got out to check," she explained defensively. "That involved a walk around the car. I couldn't help that it was 5:00 p.m., or that Ethan was watching from his patrol car. He misunderstood what he saw."

Bailey laughed and drew out of his arms. "I'll keep her in line. Don't worry."

Jeff rolled his eyes. "As long as she doesn't follow her into a fabric store. Then we'll never see either of them again."

"And that would be a bad thing, how?" Matt asked.

He was booed back onto the porch steps as both cars headed for the road. Justin and Jeff honked horns and waved.

"What a wonderful resource for you," Bailey said as they drove back to town on the dark little road.

No one knew that better than he did. "I know. That's why I came home."

"And you get along so well."

"Not always," he disputed, "but usually." He glanced at her quickly, just as the ray of light from a passing car lit her features. She looked serious. After the high spirits of their afternoon, he wondered if she'd been more affected by Willie's behavior than he'd realized.

"Willie'll get used to you," he said, watching the road. "She's probably jealous of your cookies. I had to fight to get one."

"Fortunately for you," she said lazily, "I left a tin at home. I'm sure Willie just loves you and doesn't trust me not to hurt you."

He thought wryly that he didn't, either, but didn't bother to share that with her.

"Willie aside, I'd say you've been accepted as a McIntyre." Before she could offer any objections, he added quickly, "I know. You're you, and the baby's half you, so the McIntyre half isn't that important to you, but it's important to them. And it's important to me. I like knowing that Sunday dinners will continue to be fun and a welcome part of my week."

She stretched lazily and smiled. "I like that part, too. When I was a teenager, the people next door used to get together with family and friends on Wednesday nights. I'd watch the cars come and stack up in the driveway and the front of the house, with people coming out with covered casseroles and bakery boxes. You could hear them laughing all evening long, and then at about ten-thirty they'd start to leave. The men would be carrying sleeping children, and the women had foil-wrapped leftovers." She sighed. "I used to be so jealous."

"It's curious," he said, thinking about it for the first time. "Having that missing in your life hasn't made you want it. It's made you *not* want it. I wonder why that is."

"I want it ultimately," she said in the same quiet voice in which she'd recounted the story. "Just...not yet."

JEFF BACKED OFF. Bailey turned to study his profile in the dark interior of the car and thought that was the second time he'd done that. Almost as though he understood her position.

"Are you beginning to see it my way?" she asked.

He cast her a quick look as they reached the edge of Bison City's downtown. It was just a few blocks to The Way Station.

"No," he said frankly. His eyes were clear, even in the darkness. "I'll never understand that. But I'm not you.... I have a hard time remembering that. What you want for yourself is as important as what I want for us. We're two different people who happen to be sharing a child. Not very good planning on our part, but it's a little late to bemoan that now. All we can do is our best."

She subsided, feeling tired and cranky.

BAILEY WANDERED into the kitchen Monday morning to find a note from Jeff on the table telling her that he would be in the office all day and she could call him anytime if she needed anything.

All right, she thought. All day to herself. She had yogurt and cereal for breakfast and spent most of the morning cutting her fabric into squares for Josie's quilt. She moved the patterns around in different placements and finally settled on a sort of sunshine and shadow style, alternating subtle shades with darker ones to create a sunlit effect.

She began to pin them together when a light rap on the door brought her to her feet. It was Peggy with an armload of towels and a baggie of pillow mints. "When I was pregnant," she explained, walking off into the bathroom, "I was always craving chocolate. So I brought you extra."

"Thank you, Peggy." Bailey accepted the thoughtful little gift, appreciating the perks of having friends in the right places.

Peggy stopped on her way out to look over the fabric spread out on the table. "That's beautiful," she said, touching a dark green square decorated with little brown teddy bears. "For your baby?"

"For Josie's," she corrected.

"You're doing it by hand?"

Bailey nodded. "I'm not a quilt purist, I just don't have a sewing machine here."

"Want to borrow mine?" Peggy asked. "It's a small portable and it doesn't have all the fancy stitches, but it's reliable. I put patches on the kids' jeans with it, and that's about all I use it for. Eddy's off tomorrow. I'll have him bring it by."

"You're sure you won't need it?"

"I'm sure." She smiled winningly. "You can make me a quilted pillow cover or something if you feel the need to repay me."

Bailey walked her to the door. "It's a deal. You're a pal, Peggy."

Bailey had just closed the door when the telephone

rang. It was Jeff. ''Want to get your exercise in to-day,'' he asked, ''by walking to the grill for dinner?''

''I can fix something,'' she offered.

''Yeah, but this way we'll get your exercise in, too. About five-thirty?''

''Sure.''

The date made, Bailey went back to the dining table. Her incarceration in Bison City was far less painful than she'd imagined it would be. She couldn't have asked for more comfortable surround-ings, she had friends, several worthwhile projects and a man willing to take her to dinner. What more could a woman ask?

Something more, she thought later that night after Jeff had gone to his bed and she'd retired to hers. She couldn't identify precisely what it was, but *something* more.

It wasn't sex, though she was missing that at the moment. Taunting memories of the night she'd shared with Jeff claimed her attention more and more often.

She wanted more of a connection to him than she had, but she didn't want marriage. Marriage would mean she'd have to stay here, that she wouldn't be able to live and work in New York, to travel and do all the things she'd longed to do.

So, what did she want? What relationship territory lay between the friendship they were developing and marriage? Lovers? That would never work with a baby in the house. With a child depending on the relationship for physical and emotional security, love should be total, or it shouldn't be.

Rampant hormones, she decided, were making her

crazy. Things were fine the way they were. He was coming to understand—or to accept—her need for freedom, so they would make sensible, legal arrangements after Noelle was born, then she would return to New York and Jeff could resume his bachelorhood.

Yes. That would be perfect.

She turned onto her side and closed her eyes. Maybe not perfect, but the best she was likely to get.

BAILEY LOOKED HEALTHIER, Jeff thought, than she had a week ago when he'd discovered her in New York. Her cheeks were pink and her eyes bright, and though she didn't have the serene Mother Earth sort of self-satisfaction about her that Josie had, she seemed happy enough.

Seeing her at work on personal projects, he could understand the drive that made her long for New York and, ultimately, a business of her own. She worked continually.

What had once been a hundred squares of green fabric in various shades and patterns was now a single piece of evenly matched blocks formed to create the most beautiful pattern of light and shadow. He was impressed. Her next step, she said, was to combine front and back with the middle layer of batting.

Simultaneously she was designing the calendar for the Bison City babies contest, making and freezing peanut butter cookie dough for the Thanksgiving Fair, and operating as an unlicensed design consultant and general trouble-shooter for his staff.

Jeff came out of his office one afternoon just in time to see her walk through the front door with two fat sheaves of wheat about three feet tall. Following her was a teenage boy in a red Shop and Stop apron over his jeans. A fellow employee followed him, carrying two baskets of ruddy-skinned apples.

"What's this?" Jeff asked, intercepting them. He took the sheaves from Bailey, then placed them on the low table in the lobby. He had the boys put their burdens down beside it then tipped them. She thanked the boys profusely, then sent them on their way.

"Leon wants them to flank the buffet table for the Rotary Dinner tonight," she explained. Her cheeks were flushed, and the fresh smell of outdoors clung to her dark blue coat and lavender scarf. Her hair was windblown and he couldn't quell an urge to smooth it.

"I didn't know you knew Leon," he said.

Her eyes reacted to that light touch. "Sure I do. When Maureen and Peggy and I have coffee in the dining room in the afternoon, he brings us mud pie and when he has time, he sits with us."

"But he's hated all women since his divorce."

She nodded. "He told me. But he likes us."

"Why?"

"He hasn't elaborated. We just got to talking about the Thanksgiving Fair, and I said I was going to look for sheaves of wheat to decorate our booth, and he asked me to pick up a couple for him if I found them. We also have a deal with the apples. When he's finished with them, I get one of the baskets for pies and he's making brown Betty for the restaurant."

"I like the sound of that." Jeff picked up the apples. Bailey gathered up two of the sheaves and followed him to the kitchen.

Leon was small and squarely built, a hot-tempered, volatile man who'd quit on Jeff three times in the last two years. It was as though his cleverness created such pressure in him that only an occasional venting kept him from a fatal blowup.

He was ecstatic over the wheat. He carried the sheaves right into the dining room where several tables near the window were occupied in the usual early afternoon quiet. He placed them on either side of the buffet table with an apple basket at the base of each, then stepped back to examine his handiwork.

"You've outMartha'd Martha Stewart," Bailey pronounced. "I love it."

He nodded. "A few pickets or fence posts behind them would make it more perfect, but that's probably asking a little much."

"It's really not!" Bailey exclaimed, laughing. "Our booth for the fair is made of pickets. Josie's got four lengths of them that we haven't put together yet. I'll see if she can bring them by."

Leon wrapped his arms around her and pointed scornfully to Jeff. "What do you want with this guy, Bailey? Stick with me. Together we can conquer the world."

Jeff folded his arms. "Or at least decorate buffet tables."

"Thank you." Bailey kissed Leon's cheek. "But I'd have to know your back rubbing skills before I could even consider conquering the world with you."

He put a hand to his eyes. "What is it with women and back rubs?" He held up a pair of lean, long-fingered hands. "I must save these hands for art in the kitchen."

"Leon." Bailey met his eyes with a frown. "That's not a very romantic attitude. Are you really expecting to lure me away from Jeff with it?"

Leon raised his hands in a so-be-it gesture. "Fine. Fine. If you're more interested in back massage than the magic we could have made with dried flowers and found objects, then..." He seemed to be at a loss to describe what she'd be missing.

She patted his arm. "I'm sorry, Leon. When you're over seven months pregnant, a good back rub is everything."

"And Jeff gives one?"

"A mind-bending, character-weakening, fate-defying one."

"Then it's goodbye."

"Until your pickets arrive."

He hugged her again. "Bless you." He grinned at Jeff. "On the chance that you aren't aware of this, when a woman defies her fate for you, *your* fate is sealed."

Jeff took Bailey's hand. "My fate was sealed some time ago. Get to work, Leon."

On their way back to the lobby to reclaim the other sheaves of wheat, Bailey spoke under her breath. "That's why I didn't tell you about Noelle in the first place, Jeff. Your fate isn't—"

He pulled her to a stop in the hallway that led from the dining room to the lobby. "Do you really believe I would stop feeling as though my future was tied to you and this baby just because you say it isn't? The baby didn't happen just to you. Nature deigns that you carry it, but our daughter is part of me, too, and emotionally at least, I'm as affected as you are.''

He waited for the panicked look she always took on when he talked about feeling responsible for her and the baby, but it didn't happen. In fact, though she stared at him, he couldn't tell what she was feeling.

"There's no need to shout," she said finally. "She can hear you, remember? I don't think she'd like you raising your voice to me."

He closed his eyes for patience. "I'm not shouting," he said, "I'm being emphatic. Sometimes it's very hard to get through to you. Every time I think we understand each other, you say something that makes me wonder if you ever even hear me."

"I hear you," she insisted, "it's just that you're not the final authority on everything."

"I am on this."

He went to the table in the lobby, then doubled back with the sheaves of wheat toward the stairs. She hurried along beside him, one hand on her large stomach to steady the bounce caused by quick movement. "Just a minute!" she said.

He ignored her as a family of four came downstairs with a smile for them and a quick remark to Jeff about how much they were enjoying their stay. He thanked them and told them they'd find the new fall visitors' guide at the desk.

Then he started up the stairs at a slow pace so that Bailey could take his arm, though at the moment he'd have liked nothing more than to leave her in his dust.

"You made me come here, but don't think for one minute that this baby gives you authority over *me*."

He stopped at the first-floor landing and waited for her to top the last two stairs. "I don't want authority over you," he said quietly. "That's like being handed management of Mount Saint Helens or Kilauea. I just would like to see evidence that you understand that this baby is mine as well as yours and that I intend to be a part of her life."

She paused on the landing to draw a deep breath. "I *do* understand that," she said after a moment.

"Then stop saying that my fate isn't sealed. I'm a father."

"Maybe you should stop being so defensive!" Her voice rose a little. "All I meant was that you didn't have to feel your life was over."

He started up the second flight and she kept up, holding on to him. "I don't feel like it's over," he insisted. "I feel as though a great new part of it is just beginning. I'm anxious to see what she looks like. What she *is* like."

"Well, fine," she replied querulously. "So am I."

He glanced at her as they neared the top. "I hope you're wearing a different expression the first time she sees you. That one will have her begging you to let her live with me."

She looked first stricken, then angry, then both as she waited stiffly for him to open the door to the suite. She went to her room and slammed the door.

Jeff stood in the middle of his living room with her bundles of wheat, and some taunting sense of black humor reminded him of the words from the old spiritual: "We shall come rejoicing, bringing in the sheaves."

Ha.

Chapter Eight

Bailey lay awake for hours, wondering if Jeff did intend to try to take Noelle away from her when she was born. One moment she was in abject terror that he did, and the next moment she laughed at herself for even considering it. She reminded herself of all his kindnesses.

It was just that the situation was so awkward. The last stages of a woman's pregnancy should be a time of excitement, anticipation and great happiness. Sometimes she did feel those things, but they were always undermined by thoughts of laying down rules of custody, by knowing the baby would love both parents but never spend any major part of her time with them together, that she would be deprived of all the same things Bailey had so missed in her own life—only Noelle would miss them from birth.

Bailey tried to cheer herself with the thought that she would be able to return to work, to New York. She waited for the little thrill to fill her, but it didn't even appear.

She made herself think of her office, of her co-workers, of the designs with which she would open her own shop. She even put the light on, spread the designs out on her bed and looked them over. She experienced a little flicker of pride, but it wasn't enough to combat a growing sense of concern over Noelle's impending arrival.

Jeff knocked on Bailey's door at 3:30 a.m. She glared at him from the edge of the bed. He stayed in the doorway, his eyes going over her designs on the bedspread, then over her face. "I heard you moving around," he said, looking sexily rumpled in his shorts and T-shirt. It amazed her that he could be comfortable in those clothes in the cool fall temperatures.

Then she remembered the night she'd spent with him. Curling up to him had been like snuggling with an electric blanket.

"I'm sorry I disturbed you," she said shortly. The words came out sounding as abrupt and dismissing as she'd intended them.

"You didn't," he replied patiently. "I thought you might have a backache, and since you were pouting, wouldn't want to ask for a rub. So I'm here to offer one."

She felt herself bristle. "I'm not pouting. I'm just worried."

"About what?"

"You! If this baby is as spectacular as I think she's going to be, well…you're already too possessive about her. I think custody's going to become a problem."

He raised an eyebrow. "I'm her father. But I told you, if you're reasonable and cooperative, I will be, too."

She made a production of gathering up her sketches. She didn't feel reasonable. She felt grumpy and desperate for some reassurance that this would all end happily without her having to compromise what she wanted.

But even she knew that was impossible. And she was starting to worry about how *he* would feel when she walked away with their baby. That wasn't good. It wasn't good at all.

"Go away," she said. "I'm working."

He stood there for a moment while she ignored him, then she heard the door close quietly.

Oh, fine, she thought. He was forceful and insistent all the time, but this time, when she really could have used a back rub, he took no for an answer. *Wouldn't you know?* she sighed to herself. *Men.*

BAILEY AWOKE to being lightly shaken. Jeff, dressed for work, leaned over her.

"What time is it?" she asked. Josie was due at ten for more contest planning and to help Bailey peel apples. She hadn't fallen asleep until about 5:00 a.m. Her eyes felt as though they'd been brushed, and her body used as a throw toy.

"Almost nine," he said, smoothing the hair out of her eyes. "Leon's sending a waiter up with breakfast for you. Do you want me to call Josie and tell her to come later or another day?"

She pushed herself awkwardly to a sitting position. When it looked as though she wasn't going to make it, he reached under her arms and lifted her against the pillows. His thumbs grazed both breasts and it felt as though she'd touched an electric fence.

What *was* she going to do about the next six and a half weeks? If she was going to stay here, something had to change.

"No, I'll be fine." Her voice was small and froggy. "Go on."

He looked as dispirited as she felt, but much fresher.

"All right," he said, straightening. "If the situation changes and you *do* need something, you know where I am."

"Yes. Thank you."

Later that morning Josie looked at Bailey as though she was crazy, when she explained her fear about Jeff wanting to keep their baby.

"Jeff would never hurt you that way." Josie peeled a long, spiral strip off an apple, then stopped to frown at her. "He's bossy and argumentative, and sometimes he forgets that other people have opinions, too, but he isn't cruel. Even when he's angry, and even when someone else has been cruel to him, hurting them is the last thing he'd think of. Now, if someone had hurt me or one of the guys, that'd be different."

Bailey understood that. She'd seen the McIntyres in action.

Josie raised a finger for silence while she operated the garbage disposal. When the grinding had finished, she picked up a fresh apple from the basket and started peeling. "Maybe you've got a little guilt operating here," she said with a smile intended to soothe the sting of the words. "You know you should have told him about the baby so you probably think he has some right to reprisal, and in your mind the worst thing you can think of is that he'd try to take the baby. Maybe you even understand how much he cares about her.''

Bailey waved her paring knife in a broad gesture of exasperation. Josie stepped back. ''I'm confused,'' Bailey said. ''I don't know what to think. I've always been so focused on what I wanted and I'm...I'm starting to lose it.''

''It's hormones.'' Josie dropped a naked apple in the water-filled pan. ''I have strange fears and anxieties, too.'' She sighed wistfully. ''I'm terrified I'll never get my waistline back, for one.''

Bailey could have died a happy woman had that been her major concern.

''I'm also afraid my baby will hate me,'' Josie said. When Bailey protested, she insisted. ''No, it's true. I talk too much, never listen, act before I think. What kind of mother am I going to make?''

Josie thought about her own question for a moment while Bailey stood by, trying to think of a way to put a positive spin on those qualities. Then Josie grinned. ''I guess I'll be the same kind of mother I have. She's just like that, and we all adore her. Because she's real. She's not a paragon, she's a genuine woman. She loves us and that's what a baby responds to.''

How would a baby respond, Bailey wondered, to a mother who'd tried to keep her from her father?

''I think we need a tea break.'' Bailey turned on the burner under the kettle.

''That sounds good. Do you have any peanut butter cookies?'' Josie opened the cupboard over her head, pretending to snoop.

"Sorry. Jeff ate them all." Bailey reached into the cupboard over Josie's head for plates. "I do have a caramel cheesecake Leon's trying out for the restaurant, though."

"Now you're talking." Josie went to sit at the table. "Actually, I think your problem is that you're not married to Jeff. No, no," she corrected quickly when Bailey sat across from her with two pieces of cheesecake and a challenging look. "A family is still a family, even when it's loosely connected. But I meant in terms of your sense of comfort and security."

Bailey pushed a plate forward. "I used to think I didn't want or need to feel secure."

Josie looked at her doubtfully. "How can you be seven and a half months pregnant with no one else in the world, and not want security?" She narrowed her gaze on Bailey. "Of course you want security. You don't want it to confine you, which security has a tendency to do, but you want it. Don't you?"

It was a difficult thing for Bailey to admit. She remembered what it felt like when Jeff held her or touched her or even walked by her. When she moved around the apartment, he had a way of glancing at her that was proprietary, as though he was assessing her condition to see what he could do for her.

She loved that.

"Yes, I think I do," she admitted.

"See?" Josie shrugged. "We've struggled for our freedom and our rights, but you can't live without love, you can't bring children into the world without love, and love, my dear, current dogma to the contrary, is all about the surrender of self."

Bailey tapped her cheesecake with the tip of her fork. "But men have to surrender to it, too. So we're still equal in the relationship. Right?"

Josie nodded. "Yeah. Justin and I seem to be."

Bailey shook her head. "I don't know about Jeff and me. We haven't talked about love."

Josie frowned sagely. "Well, there you go. Problem identified."

JEFF CAME HOME to the wonderful aroma of something in the oven, something sweet and cinnamony. It filled the rooms and even the hallway with its cozy, homey appeal and made him feel like one of millions of nine-to-five husbands who came home to a wife and 2.3 children and an evening of domestic contentment in front of the television.

He smiled to himself as he looked around for Bailey, thinking that his situation was really far more unusual than that. How many wives today had time to bake pies from scratch?

Finding the kitchen empty, except for the pies cooling on the counter, he started across the living room toward the bedrooms, and was stopped by the sound of sobs. It was so at odds with the aroma of domestic bliss that he experienced sudden and urgent panic.

Something serious had happened to Bailey! Or the baby!

He ran the rest of the way to Bailey's room and stopped in his tracks again at the sight of her wrestling with some at-first-unidentifiable wooden object that seemed to be defying her attempts to open or close it. Legs folded on her, a hinged slab of wood dangled uselessly.

And all the while she wept like a woman who'd lost everything she had in the world.

As he went toward her, completely confused, he realized that his drafting table from the house in the Hamptons had arrived.

"Whoa," he said gently, disentangling her from the folding legs that seemed determined to beat her into submission. He opened the legs out, swung the slice of wood that became the tabletop in the direction opposite the one she'd been trying to force, and the table was ready for use.

She sank onto the edge of the bed, still sobbing, her face in her hands.

He felt uncharacteristically helpless. She was often argumentative, smart-mouthed, and sometimes even deliberately difficult, but he'd never seen her hysterical. He sat down beside her and put an arm around her.

She leaned into him, her whole body racked by her sobs. He held her closer, and instinctively put a hand to the baby, certain this had to be upsetting her if she truly could hear everything.

"Bailey, what is it?" he asked

"It's everything!" she wept. Then she added in a high squeak, "Everything. Everything."

He rocked her and rubbed the shoulder he held. "Like what, specifically?"

She raised her head from his shoulder to look into his face. Her eyes were truly anguished and miserable. "What *isn't* wrong here, Jeff?" she demanded. "We have a baby on the way who's going to have

a different last name from mine on her birth certifi-
cate, and not because her mother has an independent
streak, but because she isn't married to the baby's
father! I had thought that could be okay, but how can
it? I mean, Noelle's going to run up frequent-flier
miles like a Microsoft executive because her parents
aren't a unit at all like the word implies, but two
separate people who live across the country from
each other!''

He tried to think logically and calmly. He knew
what the solution was, but he tried to analyze what
it was Bailey wanted to hear. She wanted to know
everything would be all right. Who didn't?

''I know it's not ideal,'' he said. ''But lots of families operate that way and it seems to work.''

''Do you have figures, examples?''

Before he could open his mouth to reply, she forestalled him. ''Of course you don't. Because nobody
wants that as a standard. I want this baby to have
been conceived because we loved each other and
wanted a future together!''

''Yes. But we have to deal with what we've got.''
That came out sounding as lame as it felt.

''What have we got?'' she asked plaintively, her
face crumpling under a new onslaught of sobs. ''A
mother who looks like a casaba with arms and legs!
Who doesn't know what she wants!'' She looked at
him again, her eyes wide, liquid pools of sadness.
''Look at how I've screwed up all our lives!''

''Bailey.'' He tightened his grip on her. ''You
didn't do this all by yourself, remember?''

''No, but I left. I stayed away. I didn't tell you I

was pregnant.'' She pressed a shredded tissue to her red nose.

"Okay, but we've come to terms with all that."

She sniffed and drew a ragged breath. Then she asked, looking eager to believe him, "We have?"

Truth, he decided, wasn't always the best policy. Especially when a man held an hysterical woman in his arms. "I have," he said. "We're going to make it work out."

"How?"

"Through cleverness, compromise, and a mutual love for this baby." He shaped his hand to the contour of her belly. Noelle kicked the palm of his hand.

"You think so?"

"I'm sure of it." He had a sudden inspiration. He got to his feet and pulled her with him. "You need a change of scenery. Get dressed. I'm going to take you dancing."

She took a step back from him, her expression skeptical. A favorite top she wore around the house now wouldn't button over her stomach. "Look at me. I could wrestle whales, and you want to take me dancing? I don't think so."

He knew how to get to her. "I thought you wanted the baby to experience our closeness. What better way to do it than on the dance floor, in each other's arms, her between us?"

She was vacillating. "I don't know if my dress still fits."

"It doesn't matter what you wear. It's dark and intimate and the food and the music are great."

She thought hard, then relented. "Okay," she said.

"Half an hour?".

"Take your time."

BAILEY SWAYED IN Jeff's arms to the music of a bluesy rendition of "Sentimental Journey." She felt precisely as though she were on one. Just over seven months ago, she and Jeff had danced all afternoon at Josie and Justin's wedding, and that had been the prelude to the night that had brought them to this point in time.

The only trouble with this "journey" was that she didn't know if she was going forward or back. She'd been so sure that moving ahead in her life meant working in New York and eventually having her own design company. But this afternoon, before her mood had swung to depression, she'd begun thinking about the feasibility of working here by phone and fax, just as she'd done when her mother had been ill. It had worked then. She'd craved another life, but it had worked.

She'd been in Bison City less than two weeks, but already New York seemed like another planet. She'd been able to live there for a year, loved it for that time, but perhaps it was time to move on to something else.

Or was she just feeling this way because her mood had been swinging like a pendulum lately, completely disorienting her? Jeff was solid and represented the security Josie was so sure Bailey needed— that *Bailey* was beginning to think Bailey needed.

Dancing with Jeff did nothing to diminish that feeling. She could stand forever, she thought, with her arms wrapped around his middle, her body turned slightly to accommodate her stomach, his arms wrapped around her and holding her close.

She'd always been a woman who could take care of herself, but she loved the knowledge that she could give over control, even for a little while, and she would still be safe because someone else cared.

She snuggled closer to Jeff as "Sentimental Journey" turned into "As Time Goes By." "What do you think would have happened if I'd stayed?" she asked.

He ran a gentle, possessive hand up and down her back. "I like to think you'd have grown to love it here, that you'd have found a way to work that would have satisfied you and still allowed you to have your design company. That we'd have recognized our passion for each other as love and we'd be married by now, with nothing to worry about in the baby's arrival except the usual concerns about delivery."

She let herself live in that little scenario for a moment; fears about the baby's future vanished in the knowledge that Noelle's parents—together—would take care of everything.

"But the truth," he went on, a wryness in his voice, "is probably that though you love Josie and have made friends of my staff, you *wouldn't* be able to work to your full potential here as a designer, and you'd have eventually become bored and maybe bitter, and would be on your way back to New York the moment the baby was born, anyway. And you might even be more upset with me than you are now."

"Why?" She raised her head to look into his eyes. "It wouldn't be your fault. We did this together."

"I know. But that seems to be the way those things work. Or the way it is when they *don't* work. You blame the person who made you fall in love and take the chance."

She rested her head back in the hollow of his neck and shoulder. "That's awful."

"Well, the good thing," he said cheerfully, "if we want to look at it that way, is that we didn't do that. You still got what you want. Or at least you're working toward it."

"But…what did you get?"

"I've always had a lot," he said aloud. "I'm fine. And we're going to work out the custody thing, so it's going to be all right."

She didn't know how to respond to such a generous reply, so she did what she'd longed to do since he'd pulled out her chair at the tiny table in the corner of the dining room and told her she looked beautiful. She stopped moving to the music, raised her arms up to twine them around his neck and bring his lips down to hers. She kissed him deeply, fervently, longingly.

"I want to go home," she said.

He looked confused for a moment. "To New York?"

"No." She nipped at his lip, ignoring the other couples on the dance floor smiling at them. "To the suite."

JEFF GUESSED what was happening here and determined to be careful. That kiss had been enough to set his heart hammering, his body preparing for more. He'd never stopped wanting Bailey.

But though he wanted to make love to her more than anything—and he was pretty sure that was where this was going—he didn't want to take advantage of a weepy mood when she might feel differently in the morning.

He tried to engage her in conversation on the drive home, but her answers were perfunctory. She seemed more interested in stroking the baby than talking.

He was beginning to think he'd misread her completely, then he let them into the suite, and she took his hand. She headed for the bedrooms. His brain scrambled to reassess, to find his earlier thought about not wanting to take advantage of a mood swing and make himself repeat it until he believed it.

Bailey turned in the direction of his room. He pulled her to a stop. She studied him in concerned surprise. "You don't want to?"

"God." He leaned an elbow against the wall and ran a hand over his face. "Right. Like that would happen. I just think you might want to give this a little thought."

Her eyes grew languid. "It's all I've thought about since you walked into the studio that day."

"Bailey, can you trust this mood? A couple of hours ago you were sobbing, yesterday you were fighting with me. This could just be a mood you won't even recognize in the morning."

She made a small, scornful noise and walked around him to pull off his jacket. "Do you have any idea what it does to a woman when you dismiss her attempts at seduction as nothing more than a hormonal surge?" She put both hands to his back and pushed.

She was a lot smaller than he and pregnant, he told himself. If he struggled too hard, he might hurt her. So he allowed himself to be shoved into his bedroom. It was dark and cool and smelled of the detergent and softener Peggy used on the hotel's linens.

He turned to her at the side of the bed, his index finger raised to make a point. "Bailey, you should—"

She caught his finger and bit it.

"Ow!" he complained on a laugh.

"You said you didn't want to run my life," she reminded him.

"I don't," he insisted, shaking the pain away. "But how safe would this be, anyway?" He caught her hand as she tried to unbutton his shirt. "And not only physically. I don't want you to think you can run in and out of my life as though nothing of signi—"

She kissed him into silence. "Did I say anything about running out?" she whispered. "I'm thinking I should never have left you. Your scenario was right until you got to the bored and bitter part. I *do* love it here. I love Josie, but I really like the rest of your family, too. I love this hotel, this suite, this part of town where you can look out and see people bustling back and forth in cowboy hats and pickup trucks or business suits and Cadillacs. Whatever. I like the way I feel here."

She undid the top few buttons of his shirt and put her lips there.

He was lost. He abandoned all his arguments and his attempt to be noble and gave himself over to the seduction she was so determined to complete. He wondered if she had any idea how easy that would be from here on out.

BAILEY WAS DRUNK WITH POWER. The moment the resistance in Jeff's eyes turned to compliance, she began to feel that *finally* all was right with her world. He helped her pull his shirt out of the waistband of his pants, then leaned over to flip on the bedside light.

He turned her around and unzipped her dress, then spun her to him again and tried to pull the now-loose spaghetti straps off her shoulders. But she held the fabric to her breasts with one hand and turned off the light with the other.

"We have to do this in the dark," she said, her voice laced with humor, "or you might not be able to go through with it. I'm all veiny and kind of..."

He put the light on again and, with a scolding frown, pulled her hand away from the front of her dress. It fell to her stomach. He pulled it off over her head, then did the same with the slip underneath.

She stood in white cotton bra and panties, round and ripe and pink-cheeked. He wasn't sure if the blush meant indignation or embarrassment. "The last time we did this," she said in a small voice, "I'd been dieting and exercising to be gorgeous in my bridesmaid dress. I was—"

He nodded, reaching around her to unhook her bra. He tossed it to the chair with the dress and slip. "I thought you were the prettiest thing I'd ever seen," he said, shaping her round, swollen breasts in his hands. He loved the weight of them and the knowledge that what they'd created together made her this way.

He leaned down to kiss her. ''But I think you're even more beautiful now,'' he said against her lips. ''You're talking about staying instead of leaving.''

She wrapped her arms around his neck. ''Oh, Jeff,'' she whispered. ''I'm so sorry I hurt you.''

He lifted her onto the bed and leaned over her. ''You're doing a wonderful job of making it up to me,'' he said, then pulled her cotton panties off. He found her belly beautiful with life stirring inside it. He stroked it gently and shook his head. ''Boggles your mind, doesn't it?''

BAILEY THOUGHT that *he* was the one boggling her mind at the moment. He'd made her feel very special this evening when he tried to comfort her, then he'd made her feel beautiful and seductive when he'd danced with her. Now he was revering her as though she were some goddess.

Self-consciousness over her bulbous proportions fled and all she wanted was to make love with him— even with the light on.

She patted the bed beside her. ''You're still dressed,'' she said. ''I'd sit up to rectify that, but I don't think I can. So you'll have to come down to me.'' He reached for his belt buckle as he walked around the bed, but she stopped him with a smile. ''No, Jeff. I'd like to do that.''

He sat down, pulled off his shoes, then lay beside her, apparently eager to let her have her way with him. She unbuckled his belt, unbuttoned and unzipped his pants, then struggled to her knees to pull them and his shorts off.

He drew her down into his arms, and for a moment they just held each other, relishing the silky-rough, flesh-to-flesh contact. She ran her foot up his leg and held him close. His hands roamed her body as he whispered her name. "It feels like a lifetime since I last held you."

She kissed his throat. "I know. I missed you so much. I didn't want to, I told myself I didn't need you, but every night, there you were...living in my mind."

His hand went down her back, over her bottom, then up again with a slight detour to the inside of her leg. She felt her blood rushing through her, her heart pounding, her body in waiting mode; tension stretched as she waited for his touch where he seemed most determined to ignore her.

Her hands ran over his chest, his strong rib cage, his flat stomach. He tried to prevent her from reaching lower but he was too late.

WHITE-HOT FEELING erupted inside him and radiated to every extremity. Jeff had to make a conscious effort to think. He wanted to extend her pleasure for her. He'd heard friends talk. Sometimes pregnancy didn't permit orgasm and he wanted...

She didn't seem to care what he wanted, but was going in direct pursuit of what *she* wanted.

"We have to remember what— Ah, Bailey. What Dr. Elizabeth said." He caught her hands in his and drew her over him. "Easy. We have to—" He gasped as she pulled one hand free and ignored him.

"Bedside table," he said urgently while he could still form a coherent thought. "Condoms in the…" He pointed.

She reached for one, kissed him soundly, then laughed. "Hopefully, this one's more dependable than the last one."

He pulled her astride him. "Just hurry up and…"

She put it on him, and then he lost awareness of everything but her. She enfolded him, surrounded him, became every single particle of his world.

BAILEY CAME TO CLIMAX almost instantly. She tried to take him deeper, but Jeff held her hips and boosted her up to prevent it. Still the delicious friction and, she guessed, the unutterable tenderness with which he was determined to comply with the doctor's instructions for her safety, brought her to rich fulfillment.

He followed, his body's tremors in time with hers, and she discovered a self-satisfaction that existed outside of her own pleasure. She was huge and weirdly shaped, but he seemed to treasure her even more than he had when they'd conceived Noelle.

Then he'd been tender and caring and everything wonderful a woman looks for in a lover, but he'd been so in charge. The night had been a marathon of passion and excitement.

But this time he was less in charge and more in tune, as though they'd reached a true sharing of the experience. This time, she felt, she'd done as much for him as he had for her. It made her feel powerful.

As the world began to settle around them, she moved on him again, ignoring his protests. Whatever they were, he didn't make them very clear, and she removed the old condom, applied a new one and finally silenced him with her body.

Sometime later they showered together, ate cheesecake and milk while wrapped in robes in the dark kitchen, then curled up together in the middle of his bed and went to sleep, Noelle quiet between them.

Chapter Nine

Life settled into a comfortable domestic routine in the week that followed. Jeff and Bailey walked a mile every morning before breakfast. Fall colors in the aspens and cottonwoods around town grew more rusty with the approach of winter, and a chilling morning fog often lay in the folds of the mountains like a length of gauze.

Bailey absorbed the beauty of her surroundings as she walked along, her arm tucked into Jeff's, convinced the baby was taking it all in and feeling her mother's happiness and contentment.

She attached batting to the underside of the squares she'd sewn together for Josie, applied the back and was busy making the binding in a solid dark green. But it was getting harder and harder to find time for the project as the Thanksgiving Fair drew closer. Josie's and her major push for the Millennium Baby contest was aimed at that and there were a million details to see to.

She and Jeff designed tickets and flyers, prepared the newspaper ads with help from Justin—and expended major energy on avoiding a discussion about the details of their future.

But their need to address the issue came to a head after Sunday dinner at the ranch. Matt had built Josie and Bailey a booth out of old fencing, and they'd retreated to a corner of the barn to decorate it while the men watched football.

Bailey stood on a short ladder, hot-gluing large gold foil stars to the outside of the booth. Into the center of each star would go one of the many pictures of babies that she and Josie had cut out of magazines.

Josie peered up at the booth, hands on her hips, and frowned. "The sign's crooked," she said.

Bailey climbed down off the ladder and went to stand beside her. They'd made an oblong sign with gold ink on black poster board. It read "Bison City's" in small print, then "Millennium Babies" in large script with stars dotting the *i*s and bordering the sign. Josie was right. It listed seriously to the right.

"I'll fix it." Bailey climbed the ladder again, having to go to the very top this time to pull out the tacks that held the sign in place.

Josie stood under her, arms raised toward her. "Bailey, we can let one of the guys do it. You shouldn't be up that high."

"I'm fine," Bailey insisted. "My footing's solid, so don't worry. Step back and see how this looks." She held the sign in place.

Josie did as she asked. "I think it's all right." She laughed. "I'm not sure, though. You take up a lot of my field of vision."

Bailey looked over her shoulder and made a face

at Josie. "I don't know if you've noticed, but you're a little blimpy yourself, Babar."

Josie came to the ladder and swatted her foot. "No point in being nasty. Hurry up with that. You're making me nervous."

Bailey reapplied the tacks on the top of the sign, and was about to lean out a little to put in the bottom one on the far left when her right wrist was trapped in a firm grip. She turned her head in surprise and found herself face-to-face with Jeff, who stood a step below her. His expression was dark with displeasure.

He took a step down, urging her to follow. "Come down," he said, his voice quietly stiff.

Carefully balanced, her left hand holding the top of the booth, she pulled against him. "Jeff, I'm not finished. The sign was—"

"Come down," he repeated, then added with unabashed authority, "now."

She raised an eyebrow at his tone, then copied it. "Let me go," she said. "Now."

"You should not be on top of a ladder!" His voice rose a decibel.

She remained calm. "My footing's solid. I'm—"

"I'll finish for you." He interrupted her with strained patience. "Get down."

"When I'm finished!"

"Bailey..." Josie began hesitantly.

Bailey thought she'd won the minor skirmish when Jeff went down another step, but his well-timed tug pitched her awkwardly sideways, into his arms.

Josie gasped and another male voice shouted. Bailey hadn't realized Matt was there until she was placed on her feet beside him.

He put his hands out to steady her, but Jeff caught her arm and spun her toward him. "What is *wrong* with you? You're seven and a half months pregnant! You do not belong on top of a ladder!"

Every instinct for freedom Bailey had suppressed in the interest of living in peace with this man until her baby was born erupted as though shot with a sling.

"I belong wherever the hell I choose to be! I was perfectly safe!"

"You can't even walk across our living room without colliding with something!"

"I was holding on!"

"It's a four-foot drop!"

"I didn't intend to fall!"

"You had thirty pounds attached to the front of you hanging out in midair! One wrong move and you wouldn't have been able to stop yourself!"

She stared back at him pugnaciously, tears standing in her eyes and an enraged bellow on the tip of her tongue. But she held both back with determined will. It was the thirty pounds that did it. It wasn't the issue here, of course, but it was a good excuse for the tears.

"I've only gained twenty-one, thank you very much," she said with injured dignity and turned for the door.

He caught her arm. "No, you don't."

"Jeff!" Josie said sharply. "She didn't—"

He turned on her. "And what's the matter with you, anyway? Why didn't you stop her?"

"She was—" Josie tried to answer.

"I swear, sometimes you show no more sense than you did when you were twelve!"

"Don't you dare yell at me! I'm no longer just the little sister you can ignore unless you need someone to shout at!"

"Hey!" Matt stood between them, arms held out as though he expected to have to part them physically at any moment. "We're deteriorating into a bad talk show segment here. Let's just calm down, okay?"

The moment quiet fell, Bailey yanked out of Jeff's grip and headed for the door.

JEFF, DISTRACTED by Matt's interference and Josie's surprisingly hot anger, allowed Bailey to break free of him. He started after her, but Matt stopped him.

With a glower at Jeff, Josie waddled after Bailey.

Jeff bristled. "This is not your business," he warned Matt.

Matt appeared unimpressed. "Everybody in this family is my business," he said calmly. "I know. Technically, she's not a McIntyre, but she's carrying one, so that changes things. She probably wasn't thinking when she climbed the ladder. I know she scared you, but yelling's not going to erase the fear."

"It was a foolish thing to do!"

He conceded that with a nod. "She loves you. She seems prone to behaving foolishly."

Jeff tried to walk away. Matt held on. "Just one more thing," he said. "Something you have to come to terms with now—especially with a child coming."

"What?" Jeff asked irritably. "She's going to have a meddlesome uncle?"

He conceded that, too. "Yes. And when you love

someone as much as you love your woman and your child, a part of you is in terror your whole life because of what could happen to them when you're not there to stand between them and danger. But don't blame them for it. It comes with the job.''

In Matt's case neither determination nor valor had been able to protect his family from danger. He'd lost them to one of the nameless fears he spoke of. That was why, Jeff told himself, he let Matt talk to him that way. Not because he made sense.

''And if you're hoping for any peace in the future,'' Matt went on, climbing the ladder and putting the last few tacks in place, ''you'd better apologize to Josie right after you apologize to Bailey.''

''She—''

''Doesn't matter. And I'd hate to see Justin kill you for making her cry.'' He looked at Jeff over his shoulder. ''How's it look?''

Jeff sighed at the memory of how simple his life used to be. Then he looked up at the sign. ''It's crooked,'' he said.

BAILEY DIDN'T SPEAK TO HIM all the way home. She sat in her seat belt like something trapped and stared dispiritedly at the passing landscape.

''I'm sorry I shouted at you,'' he said finally as they approached the outskirts of town. ''But I about had a stroke when I walked into the barn and saw you standing on the top of the ladder. You're not even supposed to stand on the top step of a ladder when you're *not* pregnant.''

She gave him a cutting look, but said nothing. That was similar to the reaction he'd gotten from Josie when he'd tracked her down in the kitchen pulling a carton of fudgey rocky-road out of the freezer.

But he knew how to get Bailey to talk.

"We have to discuss the wedding sometime," he said, pulling up at the stop sign. He kept his eyes on the road.

He felt Bailey's startled breath when she turned to him. "Whose wedding?"

He looked both ways then proceeded. "Our wedding. You're staying, remember?"

Eyes studiously trained on the nearly nonexistent Sunday afternoon traffic, he couldn't see what she was doing. But he could imagine. He was being treated to the imperious-duchess look, followed by the are-you-out-of-your-mind look.

"I said I was staying," she said in the imperious-duchess voice. "Not that I was marrying you."

"Then, what are you going to do?" He supposed he shouldn't even ask at this point, but he was trying to get a dialogue going.

He turned up the street to Way Station Road. He heard her scornful little gasp. "After your little display in the barn, I'm on the brink of changing my mind about everything."

He'd known since he'd yanked her off the ladder that that possibility existed, and he was frightened of it, but he pretended he still had the upper hand.

"Then I'd have to change my mind about taking you to court, wouldn't I?" He made the threat casually as he drove a block past The Way Station and turned into his marked spot in the parking lot.

She stared at him as he turned off the ignition and

removed the key. When he met her eyes, he made sure there was ruthless determination in them.

She saw it there. He could tell by the way she drew back from him. But she looked more studious than panicky as she stared at him. "I'm no longer convinced you'd do that," she said finally.

He opened his door. "Then you'll be rudely surprised." He slammed it closed then walked around her side to help her out.

She looked up at him, a small smirk in place. "Yeah." She took both hands he offered and pulled herself up. She bumped him with her belly, a touch that always melted him to mush. He had to concentrate to keep the threat on his face. "You'd like me to think you're so ruthless, wouldn't you?"

"Who won the ladder incident?" he asked.

She shook her head at him, the sadness returning to her eyes. "Neither one of us. You don't think you won because you had the muscle to make me do what you wanted?"

"I had the muscle to get you out of danger," he corrected. "*That* was what I wanted."

She rolled her eyes and pulled away from him, intending to stalk to the back door of the hotel. But stalking in her advanced stage of pregnancy lost all its ability to impress when everything between her chin and her knees swayed. He caught up with her in four strides.

She stopped to face him before they went inside. "I knew what I wanted before you walked back into my life. I wish you'd never come to New York."

He pulled the door open, clearly skeptical of her claim. "You still know what you want." He pointed a thumb at his chest. "Me. You just don't know what to do about it, because then you'd actually have to stop and make some compromises."

"You'd like to believe I want you."

"I would," he admitted, ushering her in before him. "Then I wouldn't feel so unjustified in loving *you*."

AS ANNOYED AS BAILEY WAS with him, she loved hearing that he loved her. And though she maintained a cool distance between them as they climbed the stairs, waved at the workers hanging thick cable beyond the elevator barricade on the second floor, then continued on to Jeff's suite, the words played over and over in her head.

"If you loved me," she said as he unlocked the door and pushed it open, "you'd give me some credit for good sense. I was well balanced on the ladder."

"Standing on the top of the ladder did not show good sense." He pitched his keys at a bowl on a table near the door. "And if you loved me, you'd think twice before doing whatever the hell it is you want to do in the name of this freedom you're so determined to have. Everything you do affects me and *my* freedom-from-stress."

"Why?" she demanded. "Why can't you just trust me to know what I'm doing for myself and the baby?"

He put a hand to her stomach. "Because I'm responsible for you and for her. And as long as she's tucked inside you, I'll worry about both of you."

She removed his hand. "You just want this baby.

I, unfortunately, happen to be the packaging that comes with it.''

He gave her the scolding look that remark deserved. ''That's a crock, and you know it. You'd like to think you have no value to me because that would let you off the hook. You wouldn't owe me anything for the part of your pregnancy I missed, and you wouldn't owe me a part of your future. But you do.'' He jabbed an index finger at her. ''You do. And I'm going to collect.''

She went to hang up her coat. ''I didn't know love was about 'collecting.''' She slammed the closet door.

''You've never mentioned love,'' he said, going into the kitchen to fill the kettle. ''At least not in reference to me. So you wouldn't know what it's about.''

''I *made* love with you,'' she reminded him a little hotly. She couldn't say it, but it sure as hell didn't diminish the intensity with which she felt it. ''Don't actions speak louder than words?''

He put the kettle on the burner and turned it on. ''Not in your case.'' He came halfway back toward her, hands resting loosely on his hips. ''You made love with me once before and walked away, anyway. Remember?''

She opened her mouth to offer a rebuttal, then closed it again. She had no defense.

''I'm going to take a bath,'' she said stiffly, ''and go to bed early.''

''I thought freedom was running to things,'' he said, ''not *from* things.''

She turned and walked away, finding him just too exasperating to deal with.

He brought her a cup of tea and placed it on the wide lip of the tub, then left again without a word.

Bailey sank into the bubbles, deciding that this was all Josie's fault. If Josie had gone to another college, Bailey might never have met her, made a friend of her and been invited to Wyoming as a part of the wedding where she met Jeff. If it wasn't for Josie, Bailey could be happy in New York.

Now she'd probably never be happy anywhere.

The suds were flat and the water cool almost an hour later when Bailey decided she'd indulged in self-pity long enough. But getting out of the tub was far more difficult than getting in had been.

She didn't feel steady enough to simply push up on the sides of the tub with her hands to stand, so she tried to turn onto her knees, but the tub was narrow and she wasn't.

After considering, then discarding several options, she did the only other thing she could think of. She shouted for Jeff.

He was there in an instant. She was carrying his baby and she'd made love with him just a few nights ago, but she crossed her arms over her breasts, anyway. She and Jeff were at odds, and somehow that brought about a self-conscious modesty.

"I can't get out," she announced without preamble, her earlier pride and contentiousness soaked away. "Would you help me, please?"

If he was amused, he didn't betray that to her. He planted a sneakered foot beside her thighs on the bottom of the tub, then leaned over her. "Put your arms around my neck."

"I'll break your back!" she protested.

He ignored her warning and lifted her arms around him when she wouldn't do it on her own. "Now hold on." As he drew her up, he braced one arm on the side of the tub and wrapped the other around her.

"You're getting all wet!" She knew that was a ridiculous and inconsequential observation, but she was embarrassed and regretting their earlier argument in the face of his constant willingness to help.

"That's one of the side effects of rescuing someone caught in a...bathtub." The last word came out with a grunt as he straightened up with her in one smooth but Herculean burst of muscle. Then he held on to her as she stepped over the side of the tub and onto the carpet.

He wrapped her in a thick yellow towel, letting her hold the front together while he rubbed her back through the thick terry.

"Warm enough?" he asked. He peered over her shoulder to look at her face just as she tipped it back, prepared to answer. His lips were just a half inch from hers, his eyes filled with the concern that touched her.

"Yes," she whispered.

His expression changed, and he turned her into his arms and kissed her. She felt his passion, his tenderness, his frustration and a faint anger left over from this afternoon.

He'd been right about the ladder, technically. But she'd felt secure and safe, and she was the one, after all, best equipped to determine her own safety.

Now that she was calm and had had time to think, she understood that his lifting her off the ladder had had more to do with care than control. And her reaction to him had had more to do with stubbornness than any quest for independence.

"I'm sorry about this afternoon," she said, leaning her forehead on his shoulder.

He lifted her up into his arms. "Me, too," he said, and carried her into the bedroom.

JEFF HAD NO IDEA what to do about Bailey except watch her closely, love her as much as she would allow and pray that somehow, someday, she'd be able to accept that she loved him.

Because he was convinced that she did. She might not know that was what she felt, or if she did, she just didn't want to admit it because she was afraid it might compromise her independence.

But it was there in her eyes when she looked at him, in her fingertips when she touched him, in her voice when she whispered his name.

And he took pleasure in his small victories. She now stuck her head in his office to tell him when she was going out. She and Josie were devoting most of their time to getting everything prepared for their booth in the fair the following weekend. A radio spot could be heard morning and evening, urging proud parents-to-be to sign up their millennium baby in the contest.

When Jeff came upstairs at the end of the day, the aromas of dinner tantalized him.

Evenings Bailey sat with him on the sofa, Josie's quilt in her lap while she drove a lethal-looking needle threaded with a narrow gold ribbon through the corners of every block, then tied the ends into a bow. She intended to give the quilt to Josie and Justin on Thanksgiving.

She seemed eager to do everything she could for Jeff except tell him that she loved him. He decided he could live with that until he made her feel it so strongly she would have to say it or burst.

The morning of the fair he and Justin were conscripted to help set up the booth. Jeff and Bailey and Justin and Josie met early in town at the Chuck Wagon Café for breakfast, then went to the church where some hearty souls were already setting up.

By opening time, the Millennium Babies booth was the most inviting one in the hall, due in no small part, Jeff thought, to the two sparkling faces behind the counter.

He and Justin went in search of coffee.

THE MILLENNIUM BABIES BOOTH had made a tidy bundle by lunchtime. Half the pregnant women in the county had enrolled their babies in the contest, according to Annie Thatcher, Alex's girlfriend, who was part of the rotating crop of mothers-to-be who were helping man the booth.

By midafternoon, there was a lineup to buy a chance on being photographed with the Millennium Baby for the proposed calendar.

But the excitement began when a beautiful young brunette with yards of dark hair, jeans and a red-and-black buffalo-plaid shirt smiled at Bailey and Annie. Josie was taking a coffee break with Justin, and Jeff was at the ring toss.

"You look familiar," Annie said shaking her finger at the woman while she thought. "You're... ah..."

"Miranda Parker!" Bailey exclaimed, offering her hand across the counter. "From *Cheyenne News at Night!* Hi. Welcome to Bison City."

Miranda shook hands with Bailey. "Thank you." She dug into a brown leather tote and pulled out a wallet. "My crew and I are on our way home from a story in Powell, and we saw the signs for the fair and thought it might be a good place to take a break. Tell me about your booth. I noticed your ladies with signs outside the church. There are pregnant women everywhere!"

Bailey explained about the hospital and the need for extras for the new pediatrics wing. "So far, Bison City Hospital is just three rooms and a very hard-working doctor. It would be nice if our children didn't have to go to Sheridan for care."

Miranda put a ten-dollar bill on the counter. "Ten tickets, please," she said, then took out a tape recorder. "Do you mind?" she asked Bailey. "We're preparing a special segment on plans for the millennium and this would be a nice contrast to threats of the Y2K disaster."

"That'd be wonderful!" Bailey gave Annie a gentle shove. "Go find Josie." To Miranda she said, "Josie is the one who started this. Her husband is the mayor."

Miranda nodded. "Okay. But why don't you fill me in until she gets here."

Bailey told her every plan they had to make money, from enrollment in the contest to the photographs of winners for the calendar. She showed her the mockup she and Jeff had designed.

"Jeff who?" Miranda asked. "And what's Josie's last name."

"Josie Moore," Bailey answered. "And Jeff McIntyre."

Miranda blinked. "I thought Jeff McIntyre was in New York."

"He was." She knew him? "He came back several years ago."

"And you're his…?"

Bailey thought later that if Miranda had been able to give a name to what she thought Bailey was to Jeff, she might have been able to answer. But it was all so unspecific.

She patted her stomach and said the only truth she could think of. "This is his baby."

"Ohh." Miranda stretched out the word on a speculative and even calculating note, then seemed to pull herself together again. "But you're not married to him?"

"No."

"Living with him?"

Before Bailey could reply, Miranda's eyes widened and Bailey peered out the side of the booth to see Jeff and Annie and Justin and Josie coming toward them.

Miranda's expression became wistful. "How could I have ever thought that life in front of the camera was more important than that gorgeous specimen of Wyoming male?"

"Everyone knows your face now," Bailey said, part comfort, part argument.

Miranda glanced at her wistfully. "But no one knows my heart."

Then Jeff recognized her and loped the last few steps to the booth. Miranda opened her arms to him, and he leaned over her shapely frame to embrace her.

"Randy." He said the word quietly, sincerely, as though he was truly glad to see her. Then he pulled her away from him and smiled into her eyes. "You still look as though you're nineteen years old! How are you?"

Josie hovered nearby, clearly anxious to be introduced. Justin wandered to the next booth where Willie manned a wheel of fortune for the Daughters of the Pioneers. Annie returned to her place beside Bailey.

Bailey wanted to kill someone. Or at least break them in half. The feeling lasted only a moment but was violent in its intensity. She guessed that only the presence of hundreds of witnesses and the fact that she was in a church—even if it was the basement— prevented her from carrying through.

She had no right to such feelings, she told herself. She had no claim to Jeff.

But she was carrying his baby, for heaven's sake. You'd think he'd have more sense than to embrace another woman in her presence. Particularly a woman who'd been trying very hard to assess the status of his romantic involvement.

"You've met Bailey?" he asked, after he and Miranda had hugged and pulled apart again.

Bailey forced herself to smile with enthusiasm. "She wants to include us in a story she's doing on the millennium. That's why I sent Annie for Josie."

Miranda nodded. "I think our readers would like to be able to look forward to it rather than being frightened of it."

Bailey introduced Josie, and Josie, eager for the publicity, repeated everything Bailey had said, but with the inimitable Josie style.

Miranda made them all promise to wait by the booth while she went in search of her photographer. "And if any of those other pregnant ladies with the signs wander by, keep them here, too."

"This could be wonderful for us!" Josie literally rubbed her hands together in greedy anticipation of what publicity on a larger scale could mean. "We could double our baby enrollment," she said, "and maybe even double the number of people taking chances for a page on the calendar!"

Annie looked doubtful. "More publicity can't hurt, of course, but this is just Bison City. Do you really think people in Cheyenne will get as excited about it as we are?"

Josie waved away the suggestion that they wouldn't. "Of course they will. Everyone gets excited about babies." She patted her stomach, then pointed to Bailey's and Annie's. "We're excited, aren't we?"

Bailey and Annie looked at each other. Bailey didn't know Annie very well, but she did know that Alex had moved in and out of her life several times since they'd known each other and thought it unfortunate that one of the "out" times had to coincide with her pregnancy.

Bailey, on the other hand, had a McIntyre who was more than eager to be a father. She was the one who was reluctant to close off her freedom by making promises.

"I'm going to find some tea," Bailey said, raising the side closure on the booth's counter.

Annie prepared to follow her escape. "I have to go to the bathroom."

Josie pushed them both back inside. "No one's leaving until we get our photos taken. Barbara! Yo, Barb!" Josie had spotted one of their sign bearers and beckoned her over. She explained about Miranda. "Find Rachel, Katie, and the Forsythe twins. Quick!"

Bailey smiled at the fact that the Forsythe twins retained their maiden names as far as the town was concerned, despite husbands and very advanced pregnancies.

Barbara, who was due early in December and very large, frowned at her. "I don't do anything quickly, but I'll try."

Miranda's photographer, a bespectacled, pony-tailed young man named Blake, pulled up several chairs. He asked Justin to sit Josie on the booth's counter, flanked her with two of the sign bearers, seated the other three, and had Annie and Bailey stand among them.

"You look like a pumpkin patch!" Justin said from the sidelines.

"Mr. Mayor." Miranda beckoned to him to crowd him in between Josie and one of the signs. "It's always good to show the mayor supports a worthy cause."

"A pumpkin patch," Jeff called out to Justin, "with Charlie Brown in it."

"I'll get you," Justin promised while smiling for the camera.

Chapter Ten

Jeff and Bailey had dinner with Josie and Justin following the fair, then drove home. Jeff noticed Bailey's silence.

"You feeling all right?" he asked with a glance at her.

She seemed to have to pull herself out of her thoughts before she could reply. Then she turned to him, looking surprised. "I'm fine. Why?"

"It's not like you to be so quiet."

"I'm a little sleepy." She leaned her head back against the rest as though to prove it. "It's been a long day." She rubbed absently at her side.

"Noelle tickling your ribs again?"

"Yes. I guess she's ready for bed, too."

He wanted to believe everything was fine. The day had been fun. Most of his family had been there, with Bailey in the middle of them, seeming to enjoy them and behaving as though she belonged. Her friendship with Josie had been renewed as though the intervening years had disappeared, and because of that, Justin accepted her without qualm.

And now that Matt was satisfied that she wasn't out to get Jeff in any way, he accepted her, too.

People in town were getting to know her and seemed to like her, and she got along well with them. She was loving Bison City.

She just couldn't love him. Or, rather, *let* herself love him. He was sure she wanted to.

Last Sunday he'd forgotten his resolution to apply no pressure on her. He'd slipped back into his old man-of-the-West personality when he'd seen her standing on the ladder. He had to do better.

That decided, he locked up the suite while she changed for bed, then walked into his room, expecting to find her there. They'd been sharing his room since that first lovemaking.

He went to investigate and found her folding back the blankets in her room.

He instantly forgot his logically made decision. "What are you doing in here?" he asked from the doorway.

She turned with a start. She did look tired. "It's probably better," she said, rubbing her side as she slapped her pillow, one-handed.

"For whom?"

"For you," she said. "The baby's restless. I'll probably be up and down a lot."

"She usually calms down when we're in bed." He went to her, intending to rub her side. But she took a step back.

He didn't like that, but he realized this wasn't about him. Something was definitely bothering her.

He sat down on the edge of her bed and drew her down beside him. "What is it?" he asked in a tone he hoped conveyed his intention to remain there until he got an answer.

"Jeff, I'm really tired," she tried to protest.

"Then stop wasting time," he insisted brutally, "and tell me what the problem is."

She looked unhappy as she accepted defeat. "Okay!" she said grumpily. "It's Miranda."

That cheered him considerably, at least for a moment. "You're jealous?" he asked with a grin.

"No," she denied instantly, then rectified that with, "Well, yes, a little. She's so pretty and so cool. But seeing her made me realize that you have a life besides me and the baby, even though you've made us your life since you found me. And it's not fair to cut you off from someone who might be able to love you…better than I can, when I can't promise what'll happen after the baby's born. We shouldn't act like it's going to be forever when we don't know that it is."

He knew that. He didn't like to be reminded of it, but he knew it. And the only way he could fight it was the McIntyre way. You simply didn't give time or thought to what you refused to allow to take place.

"Yeah, well, *I* know what's going to happen," he told her. "So, it's all right."

She eyed him exasperatedly. "You can't know the future."

He spread his hands. "You believe what you want to believe, and I'll believe what I know to be true."

She turned to him with a sigh. "And that is?"

"That the three of us are staying together."

She tried to put him on. "You're going to magically eliminate all my doubts and fears."

He shook his head. "No. But I'll hold them for you."

"You can't do that. You're born alone, and you die alone, and in between there are all kinds of things other people can't help you with."

She looked so grave he had to put an arm around her. "Bailey, what planet have you been living on? Haven't you looked around lately? That's not what it's like in the McIntyre family. That's not how it is in this town."

She put a hand to her forehead. "Maybe. I don't even know anymore. I'm confused and disoriented. It used to be so easy and so clear before you came to New York. Now I have no idea what I want." She sighed again, then corrected, "No, that isn't true. It's that I want too much. I want things that I can't have at the same time."

"Like what?"

"I want you," she said while looking right into his eyes. It took great willpower to prevent himself from whooping. "And I want my own design company. And I want the freedom to come and go as I please. And that's just not going to happen with you."

He had to give himself that one. "No, it's not."

"I know. See? Even I know that I can't have what I want. It's insane. I don't know what to do."

Neither did he. Except to just believe it would all come right. "Well, while you're mulling it over, come to bed with me and I'll rub your side and see if we can't get Noelle to sleep."

There was a plaintive plea in her eyes. She didn't

want to hurt him, but she wanted to come with him. "That's not very healthy for you."

"My great-great-grandfather gave up saddlebags of gold for my great-great-grandmother. I can give up a little peace of mind for you. Come on." He stood and took her hand and walked her to his bedroom.

IN THE MIDDLE OF JEFF'S BED they lay like spoons, his hand slowly, coaxingly rubbing the spot on her side where the baby liked to wedge her toes.

"Did you really love her?" Bailey asked, leaning into his massage. The baby had quieted.

"Miranda? I thought I did. But she got a job with the *Bugle,* and I got the job in New York, and everything else was second to that for both of us."

"Kind of like us, only in reverse."

"Kind of. Except that I didn't know what I wanted then and now I do. And that wasn't really love and this is."

Bailey reached an arm back to touch his cheek. She wanted to tell him she loved him, too. The words were on the tip of her tongue, but they wouldn't come. She felt drawn to him, bound to him, and she was sure the words would tie a double knot around her and she wouldn't even have wriggling room.

Between them Noelle moved as though she, too, felt fidgety.

"There she goes," Jeff said, moving his hand to follow what felt like the arc of a little foot. "Off your ribs, but not necessarily quiet." He continued to rub gently—the baby with one hand, Bailey's hair with another.

Bailey felt every stroke of his fingers and found herself hypnotized by the spell of their tender possession.

She wondered sleepily who wanted wriggling room, anyway.

THE MILLENNIUM BABY BUNCH, as Miranda referred to Josie and Bailey and everyone whose photo she'd taken at the fair, were on the front page of the Cheyenne paper. The caption read: "Register Your Baby with the Fine Folks of Bison City to Be the New Millennium's First Royalty." She listed the names of those in the photograph, then followed with a story explaining how the contest worked.

Maureen, Peggy and Sonny were gathered at the hotel's front desk, poring over the paper when Jeff and Bailey walked through the lobby on their Monday-morning walk. Maureen held it up. "Look!"

"Wow, front page!" Bailey exclaimed, knowing Josie would be thrilled. "Can you believe it? And nobody's eyes are closed or anything."

"That should help the cause a little," Maureen said. "In fact..." She produced a white envelope that she handed to Bailey. "A couple who just checked out asked me to give this to whoever was taking charge of the Millennium Baby purse. They want a calendar when they're ready. They were from Florida and really loved it here."

Bailey studied the envelope in amazement. "Our first mail-order order. Thanks, Maureen." She tucked it in her pocket. "We're opening a bank account today. I'll drop them a thank-you note."

When Bailey accompanied Josie to the bank later

that morning, she tried to hand over the couple's name and address as well as their check.

"I'll keep the books," Josie said, "but you handle correspondence and PR and all that, okay? I already told the postmistress to direct all mail addressed to the contest to you. You just hold the checks aside for me, we can get together once a day to exchange stuff and make sure nobody gets missed. I don't think it'll be too monumental."

Bailey received six baby registrations, thirty-seven ticket purchases for the calendar contest, and twenty-one orders for calendars the first day.

She and Josie sat at the table in the suite's kitchen and stared at the take, pleasantly surprised. "This is great!" Josie said. "Of course, this might be pretty much it. But with the calendars at seven bucks apiece, this is a little over two-hundred dollars. Not bad for outside of Bison City."

"But the Laramie and Casper papers picked up the story this morning," Bailey reminded her.

"That's great. We might get as much again."

By the middle of the week they'd invested in a formal ledger book to keep track of everything, and Josie called Justin to ask him to print more tickets. They'd tripled what they made at the fair.

Jeff created a file on the hotel's computer to help them sort information.

Josie looked a little puzzled. "Why are we getting this reaction?" she asked.

Bailey wobbled a pencil between her thumb and forefinger. "We knew in the first place that people would love anything to do with babies, and the hospital, of course, is a good cause. But I think Jeff was right about people wanting to be excited about the new millennium, to not think of it in terms of computer problems and natural disasters but...the arrival of babies. Despite all the ugliness we hear about, we're a nurturing society. We all love our babies.''

Josie nodded numbly. ''If this continues,'' she said, touching the checks and orders on the table, ''we'll be able to furnish a health sciences center!''

JEFF LOVED TO WATCH Bailey's intense involvement in the project. She spent long periods at the kitchen table logging information on paper then on the laptop he'd brought her from his office. She wrote receipts and thank-yous and kept track of postage for Josie's record of expenses. The project had become far more detailed than either had ever imagined.

He was setting Chinese takeout on the coffee table one evening while Bailey worked when the telephone rang.

She answered the cordless near her right hand.

''Hi, Yvonne!'' Her voice sounded high and light, and he saw her put her pen down and retreat into the conversation.

He knew Yvonne was the designer Bailey had worked for in New York. He tried not to resent the intrusion. He reminded himself of his resolve to apply no pressure on her, to leave his arms open so that she could fly at any time.

For a man accustomed to holding tightly to things he loved and wanted, it had been harder than he'd imagined.

Then Bailey shrieked. He juggled and lost a fortunately closed carton of *mu shu* pork, then took several steps toward her. She was staring at him, a wide smile on her face.

As his heart dribbled back to normal, he realized that whatever she'd shouted about had been good news.

"I can't believe it!" she said to Yvonne. "So when is the decision? Next Monday. Wow. That soon. Yeah. No, I'm great. Even greater now. Thanks, Yvonne."

She turned off the phone and came slowly toward him, a look of complete astonishment on her face. "I've been nominated for the Kate Greenaway Award," she said. Then she pointed to herself in wonder. "Me. Bailey Dutton."

He opened his arms to congratulate her. "Great!" She walked into them and he enfolded her. She had to turn slightly sideways to fit. "What is that, anyway?"

"It's for designers of children's clothes," she said, looking up at him, her eyes alight. "Can you believe it? I'm actually nominated."

"Of course I can believe it. I know you're brilliant."

She looked at him skeptically. "No, you don't. You think I'm foolish and reckless."

He teased her with a nod. "But brilliant. When is the winner announced?"

"On Monday."

He almost hated to ask, but kept the smile in place. "What happens if you win?"

She shook her head. "I don't think there's a chance in hell. I mean, Floria was nominated, too, and she did those harem-turn-of-the-century newsboy sort of things.''

"Harem-newsboy?'' He narrowed his gaze trying to bring into focus what that would look like.

She spread her arms out at her sides to indicate bigness. "Voluminous pants that ended in this sort of spat thing, then short jackets and roomy caps, all done in bright colors and checks. They were adorable.''

He'd have to see that to believe it. "And what did you do?''

She snatched a shrimp from the plates he'd set out and waddled off to her room. "You finish dishing up, and I'll get my briefcase to show you.''

They had a companionable evening looking over her designs. He knew less than nothing about her field, but he understood cleverness.

She ran a finger along the lines of a romper sort of thing that had straighter lines than she'd described of the harem-newsboy design "I think children can look great and still have freedom of movement. When you walked into the studio that day, we were shooting a line I designed for Yvonne called schoolyard style.''

"I'm afraid I didn't notice," he admitted. "I was too busy noticing you.''

She put the designs down and patted her stomach as she reached over it for a mouthful of rice. "You were too busy noticing Noelle.''

"No.'' He passed her a little paper cup of plum sauce. "I looked into your eyes first and all I could think about was that I'd tried for all those months to put you out of my mind and the minute I laid eyes on you I wanted you as much as I did that morning when you walked out.''

She put her fork down and stared at him, lips parted, eyes guilty. Then he remembered his promise to himself.

''Then I noticed the baby,'' he said with a smile. ''That's when I kind of lost it. I didn't see anything else in the room. I remember waving at someone who called to me, but I'm not sure who it was.''

She looked momentarily confused, as though she'd expected a different reaction. ''Um...it was Barry West.''

''Good man. He always seemed to be able to tap into whatever I had in my head and make it look just like I pictured it. I'm sure he did the same for you, even though you didn't get to see the rest of the shoot.''

''Yes.'' Her enthusiasm had deflated. ''Yvonne said the layouts are wonderful.''

Was she upset because he'd spirited her away before her work on the project had been finished? Or was she worrying about something else?

Whatever the case, he thought, she'd just been nominated for a prestigious award, and she shouldn't be thinking about anything else but that.

He poured more tea from the pot she'd brewed to accompany their Chinese dinner. ''Say you do win this award. Say the judges aren't into the harem-newsboy look. What happens then?''

She shrugged. ''Normally I'd be honored at a banquet at the Helmsley Palace.''

She'd have to go back to New York. He didn't let himself think about that one way or the other. Then she added, "But even if that snowball's chance came to pass, I wouldn't go."

He frowned at her in surprise. "Why not?"

She gave him a look that said he was silly for having to ask the question. "Well, look at me. Hang a basket under me and I could fly you to China—nonstop."

He rolled his eyes. "You're pregnant. You're supposed to look like you've got something in there."

She dunked a fried shrimp into the sauce. "I look like I have Bison City's entire next generation in here. Josie's carrying neatly, all nice and high. She doesn't look like this. And Annie's so cute it doesn't matter what her body looks like."

"I think you look wonderful," he insisted.

"You're just being gallant because you think you have to."

"Why would I think I have to?"

"Because you're probably afraid if you told me I look like an eggplant I'd take off."

He shook his head, pulling apart an egg roll and handing her half. "I know you wouldn't leave."

"Thank you. Why wouldn't I?"

"Because I'm sure by now you know I'd come after you." He smiled amiably.

She smiled, too. "You're half-right. I wouldn't leave, because we made a deal, not because I'm afraid you'd come after me. I might be more clever at eluding you than you think."

"The point," he said with mild impatience, "is that I'm being honest when I say you look wonderful. And if you win, I think we should go."

"We?"

"We. I can't let you travel that far in your condition without an escort."

"I think it's a moot point, anyway."

"There's no such thing. Life's liquid. Anything can happen."

BAILEY THOUGHT about that statement when he came to get her the following morning and walk her downstairs. "We've got some people in the lobby who'd like to talk to you."

"Who?"

"Denver television. I called Josie and Justin and asked them to meet us here. They want to talk to her, too, and I'm sure he'll want to know what's going on."

"Television!" she exclaimed in horror, dragging against him. "You mean they want us to... Oh, no. I can't possibly..."

"I thought you wanted publicity. Think of the attention TV will bring, and the money that'll result." He coaxed her toward the stairs. "This elevator's supposed to be finished tomorrow. Won't that be a blessing? I have a heart attack every time you use the stairs."

She stopped on the top step. "Jeff, I don't give a rip about the elevator. I'm worried about television cameras! If they add ten pounds, then I'll look like—"

He covered her mouth with his hand. "Please. No more fat-lady metaphors. Do you expect to promote a new baby contest whose purpose is to raise money to furnish a children's wing using a woman who looks like a supermodel? I was in advertising, Bailey.

I'm telling you it'd never work. The audience you're trying to appeal to couldn't identify. You, on the other hand, are perfect."

She closed her eyes in resignation. He lowered his hand, and she held on to him as they walked downstairs.

Josie and Justin had arrived, and Josie looked up from a conversation with a young woman in a green wool suit as Jeff and Bailey walked into the lobby. A crew was setting up cameras, lights and sound equipment. Josie excused herself and drew Bailey aside.

"You have to speak for us," she said without preamble. Her eyes were wide and pleading.

Bailey looked down at her green sweater over the black stirrups she now wore with everything because they were comfortable and they fit—a real plus at this stage of her pregnancy.

She couldn't spot them now, but she knew the sweater had some pulls and she hadn't combed her hair since she'd gotten up that morning. "Why me?" she protested quietly as the crew moved around them with lights and cables and rearranged some of the lobby's furniture. "You're the one in charge."

Josie shrugged. "Technically, maybe, but so much of what we're doing was your idea, and you always explain it so well."

"You've never heard me explain it."

"Yes, I have. And I'm the one who talks without thinking and doesn't listen, remember?" Josie took a firm grip on Bailey's arms and gave her a little shake. "Please, Bailey. We're talking about television! This could be so important! If we make a good impression…if *you* make a good impression—'' she made that subtle change with a winning smile ''—think of what we might be able to do!''

''But look at me. I'm a fright. I—''

''Are we ready?''

The woman in the suit approached them, then a young man came to attach a microphone to the turtleneck of Bailey's sweater. Bailey looked for Jeff, feeling mild panic. She spotted him with Justin and Maureen as the young woman led her toward the fireplace.

She caught his eye and he came toward her, smilingly drawing her away from the producer fussing around her.

''Do I look all right?'' she demanded under her breath, fiddling with the neck of her sweater. ''Your cowardly sister is making me do all the talking!''

He pulled her hand away from the microphone she'd almost dislodged and held it in his two, his eyes gentle. ''You look beautiful. And don't you always do all the talking?''

He smiled as he teased her, and she pursed her lips. ''You're not helping me, Jeff.''

He laughed lightly, brought her hand to his lips and kissed her knuckles. ''Sorry. I meant that you never have difficulty expressing yourself, and that's all you have to do here. Just tell them how you got the idea, and what you expect it to do for the hospital's new wing.''

''You make it sound so easy.''

''It is easy. Just pretend you're explaining it to a friend. You're the one who gave the project sparkle and made it work. You can do this. This is film, anyway. If you mess up, they'll just do it over."

"People are going to be watching me while they're having dinner!"

"Which will allow them to learn about the project and contribute money to it."

"Promise me we don't have to watch it."

"Whatever you say."

She smiled, gaining courage one moment and losing it the next. "Don't you want to sit with me?" she asked as the producer approached again.

He kissed her cheek. "I'll be right behind the camera."

"Coward," she accused as the producer sat her in a chair by the fireplace and pushed everyone back on both sides.

Jeff took his place with Josie and Justin behind the interviewer who remained off camera. One of the crew stepped in front of him, and he saw Bailey try to peer around him as the producer gave her some last-minute instruction.

Jeff took a step to the side so that he was back in her line of vision, and she seemed to relax, though not completely. But the tension, he noticed, gave her a kind of electric quality that made her vibrant as the producer stepped away from her and the lights caught her in their snare.

"Tell us how the idea for the baby contest was conceived, Bailey," the interviewer asked, then laughed. "Pun intended, of course."

Bailey smiled self-consciously. Her hair glowed under the light, Jeff noticed, and, in his observer status, he saw that her round proportions lent her an appealing sweetness.

"The credit for the project getting under way in the first place," she replied, pointing toward Josie, "goes to Josie Moore and her husband Justin, who is mayor of Bison City." She explained about Josie's wish to help the town's small hospital and Justin's willingness to be involved. "The addition's being funded by a private donation, but there are a lot of pregnant women in the area who'll be using it for their children, and Josie wanted to make sure it would have as many of the extras as a good fundraiser could provide."

"And how did you become a part of it?" the interviewer asked.

"When you're around Josie," she said with a smiling glance at her, "you get drawn into whatever she's doing. She's a considerable force."

"You say the project was born while you were having Sunday dinner at the S-J Ranch."

"That's right."

"You're a member of the McIntyre family, then?"

Jeff watched her shake her head and wished more than anything that she could have answered that question with a yes.

"I'm a friend," she replied. "Josie and I went to college together."

There was just an instant's silence, then the interviewer asked in surprise, "And that led you to move here? I understand you're a designer of children's clothes and that you've been living in New York until just recently."

She nodded calmly. "I moved here to be with my

baby's father," she replied. When the interviewer looked puzzled, she added, "He's Josie's brother, Jeff McIntyre."

"I see. So you'll be around to take advantage of this new facility, too."

Bailey smiled, and the interviewer, presuming that was an affirmative, moved on, asking Bailey to explain how the contest worked.

She explained how it was closely related to most first-of-the-new-year giveaways. "But because this new year also brings a new millennium, we wanted to do something extra special. It was Jeff's idea to focus on the fact that the babies born now will be special. The news is full of portents of doom about the millennium, but Bison City is choosing to believe that there's hope for the future— in our babies."

She paused to draw a breath. The room was silent. "So we got the idea of having mothers-to-be enroll their babies in the contest." Bailey went on to explain about the raffle and the calendar.

"I understand that the local reaction's been favorable. That's good for the hospital," the interviewer said. "Do you think it's Bison City's positive approach to the new millennium that did it?"

Bailey patted her stomach. "I think the babies did it." Jeff watched her stroke her stomach unconsciously and felt an overwhelming sense of possession at the knowledge that he'd given her that little round burden. "No matter how difficult, how frustrating or even how ordinary your own life seems, when you're expecting a baby you just know he or she is going to have all the talents you didn't have, and none of your fears. He's going to be invincible.

He's going to be able to change the world.'' Her smile widened even more. ''That's what the new millennium *should* be about. Righting all the wrongs, filling all the gaps, building all the bridges, opening all the doors we haven't gotten around to before. And realizing all the dreams. We like to think our babies will do that.''

There was silence again while everyone stared at her, then looked at one another, realizing that they'd just been privileged with a glimpse into a mother's heart.

Jeff put a hand to his own, feeling the connection, the bond that would tie him to her eternally.

The interviewer cleared her throat. ''Can you provide an address for those watching who'd like to take a chance on being a part of this calendar, or who would just like to order one? Should they send their money here to The Way Station?''

Bailey turned to Jeff. He nodded. She reeled off the address, then the telephone number.

Finally the lights and the cameras were turned off, and the crew began to pack up its gear. The producer thanked everyone for their cooperation, then talked with Bailey and Josie awhile longer.

As Justin photographed Bailey with the interviewer for a story for the *Bugle,* a young man in long, blond hair and a leather jacket presented Jeff with an envelope containing money and a sheet of paper covered with names and addresses.

''Would you enter us in the contest?'' he asked. ''I'd love to have an excuse to come back here. This place is great.''

Jeff took the envelope from him. ''Thanks,'' he

said, shaking his hand. "You don't need an excuse, just a reservation."

The young man laughed. "You're the father of that baby?" He pointed in Bailey's direction.

"Yes," Jeff replied, feeling the surge of pride that always brought him.

"Lucky man. A woman filled with love and hope is a magical thing."

Jeff accepted that with a nod. "You have one?"

The young man shook his head. "I need one. That's how I know."

Chapter Eleven

Jeff and Bailey went to the Silver Horn Grill for dinner so Bailey wouldn't even have to be near the TV. They avoided the Chuck Wagon Café, where, they knew, all the patrons would be crowded around the TV there, to get a glimpse of Bison City's now-famous face.

"I'm recording the news," Jeff told her as he helped her out of the car. "You'll have to watch it eventually. Everyone will be asking you about it."

"I probably looked like a watermelon. Or a very large avocado."

"What is this need you have to compare yourself with produce?"

She'd been regretting her appearance on camera all afternoon. "I can't believe I let Josie talk *me* into doing it. She looks like an ad for maternity clothes with her lanky body and her high carriage. I, on the other hand, look like a pregnant—".

He stopped in the middle of the parking lot and put a hand over her mouth. "If you make one more reference to your size, I swear I'll have you barred from the fabric store."

She laughed off the threat when he lowered his hand. "You couldn't do that. They love me there."

"The owner and I are on the bank's board of directors. He'll do anything I ask. And his wife's pregnant, too. He'll be sympathetic to my plight."

She frowned gravely. "That's mean." Then, as she studied him a moment, the frown turned to a smug smile. "And you're incapable of being mean. Authoritative, a little bombastic maybe, but never mean."

And while he was dealing with having been called bombastic, she waddled off in the direction of the restaurant.

BAILEY WAS HORRIFIED to discover, as she walked through the doors, that the television from the lounge had been moved into the dining room and all the patrons and staff had crowded around to watch the news.

With a groan she turned to leave but was prevented by Jeff's presence in the doorway.

"Oh, come on." He pushed her back inside, and the owner, a tall, thickly built man in a Western-cut suit, came to greet them.

"Look who's here!" he shouted, causing every head in the room to turn.

She was greeted with smiles and cheers as the crowd parted to allow her through to the room divider where the television had been placed. Matt, Josie and Justin also stood near the front.

"Jeff said you were coming," Matt said, taking her into his arms for a hug. "We thought we'd come and watch with you. Josie says you were great."

Now thoroughly embarrassed, Bailey sent Josie a condemning glance. "She'd have been great, too, if she hadn't been such a little chicken."

"It's a McIntyre policy," Matt said. "Never do what you can get someone else to do for you. Hey, Jeff."

Josie shushed everyone and drew Bailey even closer. "Look! There's The Way Station!"

With the interviewer in the foreground, an inset shot of the hotel came into focus behind her as she talked about the growing interest across the state in a contest that had begun as a small, local fund-raiser for the Bison City Hospital and was turning into something that had the interest of the entire Rocky Mountain region.

"The project was the brainchild of Josie Moore of Bison City...." There was a roar of cheers and applause that obliterated the rest of the reporter's comment.

Then Bailey's face appeared to more cheers and Josie's frantic shushing.

"...young woman who claims to reflect the perspective of the rest of her community," the reporter said as her face disappeared and Bailey's face took up the entire screen.

She covered her eyes. Then, as she heard herself speak, slowly lowered her hands until finally she stared at herself in stupefaction. Bailey almost didn't recognize the woman on the screen. In her mind's eye she saw herself as a sharply dressed woman who'd worn power suits and focused her entire being on her career in children's fashions.

But that wasn't who she was watching. The

woman on the screen, whose cheeks had plumped, whose eyes had softened and whose body—Jeff's threat couldn't apply if she just thought it—looked like an unripe pumpkin, had to be her country clone.

She ignored the body and concentrated on the face as everyone fell into complete silence around her. She heard herself talk about the contest, then describe what the people of Bison City thought about their babies and what they wanted for them. And it all came off as genuine and sincere because she'd drawn every single word from the bottom of her heart.

"The next brilliant and generous generation starts right here in Bison City," the woman on the screen said. "And the promise of the new millennium could have no better representative than the Bison City Millennium Baby."

There was a moment's silence in the room when the station went to commercial, then there were more cheers and applause.

Justin hugged her. "You got our name in there enough times that no one will forget us! I think it's time to apply for an historic downtown designation, and funding to restore the old buildings on the back street."

"We're going to make a fortune!" Josie predicted, then was immediately pressed into service by patrons wanting to donate to the cause. To no one's surprise she'd had the foresight to bring tickets with her and order blanks for calendars.

Bailey and the three men were enlisted to help, and it was an hour later before everyone was finally able to settle down to dinner.

Bailey absorbed the warmth of the citizens of Bison City. Everyone stopped by their table before leaving the restaurant and praised her for having done a wonderful job representing their community.

"So, I take it all back," Matt said to Jeff as the waitress cleared away their plates.

"Take what back?" Jeff asked.

"Everything I said about your being a dufus of the highest order. You've redeemed yourself with Bailey."

Jeff rolled his eyes. "As if a dufus of your caliber could decide such a thing."

"We've all decided," Josie said. "She's one of us."

Justin leaned toward Bailey with a conspiratorial glance over his shoulder. "Now's the time to plot your escape. You don't *want* to be one of them. Trust me on that."

Josie punched his shoulder. "You love it and you know it. I'm the best thing that ever happened to you."

Matt smiled at Bailey. "Before Josie, Justin was on the Titanic, the Hindenberg and..."

She didn't hear the rest of what he said. She'd caught Jeff's eyes across the table and saw the love and condemnation allied in them before he looked away again.

Josie reached across the table to swat at Matt, who evaded her easily because of her inability to get too close.

"I'd like to have Bailey for a sister-in-law," Josie said, undeterred by Bailey's silence.

Justin must have kicked her because she turned to look at him in surprise. "What?" she asked.

Justin cast an apologetic glance at the parties in question. "Just be quiet, okay?" he said to Josie.

"Well, it's not like I've said anything outrageous!" she protested. "They are living together."

Justin dropped the subject, so Josie was forced to, also. It wasn't until Bailey came out of the ladies' room, just before leaving, that she heard them take up the subject again as they retrieved their coats from the rack. They were hidden from her view by a cigarette machine, but she could hear them clearly.

"...be less willing to offer an opinion on Jeff and Bailey's relationship," Justin was saying.

"Bailey's my friend! I love her. What's so awful about admitting that I'd like her for a sister-in-law?"

"Nothing, except that you put them on the spot."

"What spot? They're living together."

"But not by choice necessarily. They didn't plan this baby like we did. It just happened. So they're not living together by choice, they're just...reacting to the situation."

There was a long silence, then Bailey heard Josie's sound of distress.

"I love her, too," Justin sounded as though he were commiserating. "But you can't force them into something they don't want."

"But how do you know they don't want it?"

"Well, they were living apart until Jeff bumped into her in New York. And he had to threaten her to make her come with him until the baby's born."

Josie's voice grew quiet. "But things have changed for them since he brought her home."

"Because of the baby. But a couple has to love *each other* to stay together. Come on. Put this on. I've got to stop by the paper for a minute on the way home."

"What makes you think they don't love each other?"

"Josie, I swear to God. You've got more questions than *Jeopardy*."

"I thought that was a legi..." Their voices diminished as they walked toward the cashier.

Bailey stood alone in the dim hallway thinking how strange, and how clarifying, it was to hear your life discussed by someone else. She'd already known that everything they'd said was true. But having the picture painted in someone else's voice gave her a completely new perspective.

Their baby was an error in judgment, their current status was simply a matter of convenience, and there was little hope in their future that either of those points would change.

But Jeff had said he loved her. And she loved him, though she couldn't say the words without feeling as though a door had locked behind her. That changed everything. Didn't it?

"There you are." Jeff appeared suddenly, their coats over his arm. He looked into her eyes and put a diagnostic hand to her cheek. "What's the matter? You look pale."

"I'm fine." She took her coat from him. "I'm the Bison City Millennium Baby Queen," she said, shrugging into it before he could help her. "Seeing that everybody else's baby greets the new millennium with fanfare and excitement."

"Everybody else's?" he asked, catching her arm when she tried to walk out of the restaurant.

Her eyes brimmed with tears. "Can we talk about it at home?"

For a moment she thought he was going to insist that she explain right then and there. But he pulled his own jacket on after a moment and led her from the restaurant.

Matt and Josie and Justin were waiting in the parking lot to say goodbye. Then they all headed off in their different directions.

JEFF WOULD HAVE GIVEN his entire share in the ranch to know what Bailey was thinking. There was a frown on her brow and a distant look in her eyes, as though she was concentrating on something far and away from the interior of his van—and she didn't like what she was seeing. Whatever it was, she didn't want to talk about it until they got home.

He wondered if there was another woman in the world who worried about as many different things as she did. And if there *was* one, if she brought her man to the edge of panic as often as Jeff found himself there.

The lobby was in an uproar when they walked in. Not only was the staff excited about Bailey's appearance on TV, but many of the guests were gathered around the new elevator.

Buddy Marsh polished the cage lovingly as Maureen led them toward it. The protective barriers had been removed and all the debris cleared away. Peggy vacuumed the carpet nearby.

Buddy shoved the polishing rag in a back pocket

and pushed the up button so that the doors parted, revealing a cubicle that would comfortably hold eight people, or six with luggage. The interior was polished oak paneling with a brass light on the wall on each side. Wine-colored carpeting covered the floor.

"Inspected and approved," Buddy said, sweeping a hand toward the inside. "We were waiting for you to be the first to ride in it, Mr. McIntyre."

Jeff was momentarily distracted from worrying about Bailey by the realization of a two-year-long dream. He'd always thought The Way Station should have an elevator, but had been doubtful about finding a company that could build one in keeping with the building's historical architecture. Finally, Bailey's arrival had forced him into finding a solution.

"It's beautiful!" Bailey exclaimed beside him, walking onto the car. "Take her up, Buddy."

"Just a minute." Jeff caught her hand and pulled her off the car. "Stay with Maureen until I've tested it."

She gave him an impatient look he was growing quite accustomed to. "Buddy just said it's been tested and approved."

He smiled. "But not by me. Wait right here. I'll be back for you. Bud?"

The man got on with him and hit the second-floor button. The car climbed up smoothly, stopped and settled, then the doors parted onto the second floor. A small crowd waited there, too, applauding as Buddy closed the doors and sent the car up to the third floor.

The doors parted on Jeff's private lobby and he laughed aloud as he realized what a blessing this was going to be for Sonny. Buddy took him down to the lobby, where they picked up Bailey and went straight to the third floor. Then he pressed the lobby button, jumped off and watched the old-fashioned indicator above the doors inch its way to the number two. Over the railing, they heard the applause of those waiting to take the elevator to the lobby.

"What an occasion," Jeff said, unlocking the door and letting Bailey in. She'd sobered again after their brief elevator ride, and she pulled off her coat and went to hang it up in the small closet off the kitchen. She reached out for Jeff's and hung it up, too.

"Sonny should be very happy," she said, crossing to the window that looked out onto the lights of Bison City. "He'll have to find another way to get his exercise."

"Maureen will have to keep sending him for doughnuts."

She turned to smile at him, arms folded. "She doesn't send him," she corrected, "he just goes. It's a subtle difference, but important."

She sat down on the wide window seat, her eyes on downtown again.

Jeff remained where he was, sensing a subtle barrier between them. And he'd promised himself he wouldn't push, would let her have her small but careful distance if that made her more comfortable.

Then the barrier crumbled to dust when she turned to him and said without preamble, "Will you marry me?"

He felt himself reel, at least internally. Externally he took several slow steps toward her and leaned a hip on the back of the sofa. "Pardon me?" he asked calmly.

"Will you marry me?" she repeated.

That was what he'd thought he'd heard, but even hearing it a second time left him with a sense of disbelief. But he knew when to take advantage of a situation. "Ah…why?"

She looked surprised by the question and even a little horrified. "Why? I thought you wanted to marry me."

"I do," he admitted. "But you haven't wanted to marry me. What happened?"

She angled her chin and looked as though she would either slug him or march off as far away from him as she could get. Then all the huff seemed to go out of her, and her eyes brimmed with tears.

"Because I don't ever want our baby to feel as though her birth was a mistake," she said. "That's why."

Her eyes were dark with worry—not at all the expression that should accompany a proposal of marriage.

"What made you start thinking about the baby as a mistake?" He winced while using the word. "I thought you wanted it, even before you knew I did, too."

She met his eyes reluctantly. "I overheard Josie and Justin talking," she said. "They meant no harm, but Justin was scolding Josie for saying she wanted me for a sister-in-law, and he said that she was putting us on the spot because we hadn't planned the baby, we were just—" her mouth worked unsteadily and he took her hand "—just reacting to the situation. And I got to thinking, if we just stay together until she's born, then draw up legal documents over custody like she was some time-share property or something, then…'' A single tear fell. ''We are just reacting to the fact that I'm pregnant, and she won't feel welcome at all.''

''Okay, well that's completely wrong,'' he said, rubbing her tear away with his thumb and pulling her into his arm.

''No, it's not. We—''

''It's wrong,'' he interrupted, ''for a couple of reasons. Noelle is not a mistake. It's true that I didn't really expect her, but that night after the wedding, I was so taken with you that my total purpose was to make serious, significant love to you, and by the time we were finished, I was in love with you. My intention was to give you my heart and soul and I did.'' He smiled as she drew away to look at him. There was a little pleat between her eyes as though she didn't recognize him. ''It's just that I did it physically as well as emotionally and spiritually.''

She leaned into him as she said his name on a broken little breath. Then she straightened abruptly and looked into his eyes. ''That was wonderful to hear, Jeff, but are you saying you don't want to marry me?''

He returned her honest gaze, wondering just how far he dared push this. She had to know what she felt for him—to admit it to herself—or it would never work.

He drew a breath and took the chance. ''Not if you're asking me just for Noelle's sake. I loved you before I loved her.''

Bailey wondered if she was losing her mind. Where *had* this man come from that he could be offered what he claimed to be his heart's desire and refuse it because he didn't like the reason it was offered?

But even in her exasperation, she was touched and humbled by his declaration. And she wondered what woman in her right mind would ever *want* to be free of such a man.

"I've loved you since that weekend of the wedding," she said, tears burning her eyes, her fist clutching the front of his shirt. "You changed something in me that will never be whole without you. You made me need you when I didn't want to answer to anyone or be responsible for anyone for a long, long time."

He closed his eyes for a moment as though absorbing the words, but when he opened them again, his expression was grave. "But you haven't changed your mind about that."

She didn't have to give that much thought. The honest truth was that love was a circle and she'd never been able to make the ends come together because she'd had to have that opening for escape.

She tried to think now about where she would go if she could, but her mind was filled with Jeff and his family and Bison City and its people. And all the babies on their way.

She'd taken the bold step of proposing by telling herself she was doing it for their baby, and Jeff was making her rethink it—leaving that space open in the circle so that she could fly.

It was an odd moment, she thought with a fatalistic

smile, to realize she didn't want escape. And with that admission came a lifting of the burden of keeping her options open.

She didn't want them open. She wanted them sealed with Jeff's promise.

She looped her arms around his neck and kissed his mouth. "Actually, I have. You've succeeded in making me want you more than I want to be free. Does that scare *you?*"

He looked at her as though he'd been given all the gold Great-great-grandfather Samuel had lost. Her heart melted.

"McIntyres aren't afraid of anything," he said, crushing her to him as closely as Noelle would allow. "I knew we'd come together, I just thought you'd put me through a lot more before we got there. I love you, Bailey."

Bailey put a hand to her heart, feeling as though Noelle pushed against it with her foot. "Oh, Jeff. I love you, too."

"So, when do you want to do this?" he asked, stroking her hair from her cheek, fully expecting the moment to blow up in his arms—to learn that she'd changed her mind or that he'd been dreaming or that the mushrooms on his steak had been hallucinogenic.

But she simply drew back enough to look up at him and smile. "I'll be forever an outcast if we don't wait for your parents to get here. They're coming for Christmas, aren't they?"

He nodded. "That's cutting it a little close, isn't it? The baby's due on Christmas Day."

"I'm holding out until 12:01 a.m. on January

first,'' she said, as though she thought she could do it. "We're going to have the Millennium Baby."

He laughed. "And you're going to be able to plan a wedding *and* keep a handle on the contest and give birth all at the same time?"

"We could just have the reception right here, couldn't we?" she asked. "Just your family and the staff?"

"We'll have to sedate my mother. Matt and Josie both had big weddings."

"But big weddings take time to plan."

"Then family and staff it is. Tomorrow after your doctor's appointment, we'll get a ring."

She tried to argue, but he forestalled her by taking her to bed.

Later he lay there with her wrapped in his arms, and instead of feeling triumphant he worried about how to hold on to this sudden bounty.

He sighed into the darkness, thinking that he'd never understood that be-careful-what-you-wish-for adage until that moment. Proving oneself equal to a wish's fulfillment was a humbling exercise.

Chapter Twelve

Bailey sorted through the pile of mail in the middle of the dining room table with a one-and-a-half-carat diamond set in a little ellipse of gold on the ring finger of her left hand. Thanksgiving had come and gone and the little green quilt was now installed in the cradle Justin and Josie had found at an antique shop for their baby.

It had been four days since the telecast, and mail was coming in from all over the western United States. There were at least one hundred pieces on the table.

"It's coming too fast," Bailey repeated to Josie for the fourth time. She knew Josie's mind was on planning a combined bridal, baby shower. "It's going to be Christmas before you know it, and you said you always help Willie with cookies and preparations. Plus, your folks will be arriving, and you and I are going to have to start giving serious thought to being ready for our *own* babies as well as our Millennium Baby."

Josie dismissed that careful reasoning with the swish of an envelope postmarked Hallelujah Junction, California. "There's always time to get a few friends together. We're doing it next Friday in the banquet room. Leon's taking care of food and favors."

"Josie..."

"It's already planned." Josie slit the envelope open with a butter knife, then pretended to threaten Bailey with it. "I don't want to hear another word about it."

"But I have no family here to—"

Josie drew in an indignant gasp. "Bite your tongue! You're about to become a McIntyre! You have family coming out of the woodwork, your ears and possibly even the closet. And besides them you have all the friends you've made in town. I'm planning on forty-seven women."

Bailey stared at her in astonishment. She was sure she didn't know that many people.

"Josie, they don't *really* know me. And you'll make them feel like they have to bring a gift!"

Josie looked at her as though she'd suddenly turned green. "Well, of course they have to bring a gift. That's what showers are all about."

Bailey decided that argument was futile and concentrated on the orders for tickets and calendars that covered the table.

Later that afternoon they stared at the day's tally. Bailey blinked and looked again. "Two thousand, three hundred and fifty-seven dollars today alone!"

"Nine hundred yesterday," Josie said, studying the neat stacks of checks, money orders and cash. "I didn't think we'd get such interest out of the area." She patted Bailey's shoulder. "You're the one who did it with that dewy-eyed talk about what we want for our babies. Now you've got everybody believing in it.''

''I was not dewy-eyed,'' Bailey objected.

''You were, too,'' Josie insisted. ''You kept looking at Jeff and getting all sweet and wife-and-mothery.''

''You're ridiculous.''

Josie gave her shoulders a squeeze. ''It's the company I keep. Let's go down to the dining room and see if Leon has anything we can sample.''

Bailey was about to agree with that suggestion when the telephone rang. Josie went for her purse on the sofa while Bailey dug through the rubble of envelopes for the cordless.

It was Yvonne.

''You won,'' she announced abruptly.

''Won what?'' Bailey asked, everything else forgotten in her impending marriage and the overwhelming response to the contest.

There was a moment's silence, then Yvonne replied with indulgent impatience, ''The Kate Greenaway Award, you goose. How could you have forgotten?''

For a moment Bailey couldn't speak. She simply stared at Josie, unable to absorb the fact that she'd won the children's clothing industry's highest award for design.

Josie came to her with a frown, shouldering her purse. ''What? Bad news?''

Bailey shook her head, trying to concentrate on what Yvonne was telling her.

''...that charming little backwoods place, but, darling, you really have to come,'' she was saying. ''You can't be honored in this way and not appear to accept the award. They're putting winners up at the Pierre. Shall I tell them to include you? It's on Saturday night. You should be here Friday.''

Bailey's brain began to function. Jeff had said he'd accompany her to New York if she won.

''Please,'' she replied, excitement soaring in her— or was that Noelle's foot? ''And tell them I'm bringing my fiancé.''

''Fiancé.'' Yvonne sighed. ''Oh, no. This means you're never coming back, doesn't it?''

''Just to accept the occasional award,'' Bailey teased. ''Thanks, Yvonne. I'll see you Friday.''

Josie was as excited as Bailey when Bailey explained. They went down together in the elevator to tell Jeff.

''I can't believe it,'' she exclaimed, pacing his small office. ''I won. *Me!* I'm going to get the Kate Greenaway Award for Design. Do you believe it?''

''Of course I believe it.'' He stopped her and pulled her into his lap, wrapped his arms around her, smiling proudly. ''I'm probably less surprised than you are. Congratulations! That's wonderful.''

''They're putting us up at the Pierre.''

''Whoa.''

''Yeah. We're supposed to be there on Friday. The awards are the following night.''

''All right. I'll make the arrangements.''

''I've got to call Justin!'' Josie said, reaching for Jeff's phone. ''I'm sure he'll want a photo and a story. Maybe even one of your designs, if you have one with you.''

Bailey tugged Jeff out into the lobby and studied his face for any sign that his smiling pride in her was a performance. "You are really happy for me?" she asked.

He was clearly, and apparently genuinely, surprised by the question. "Why wouldn't I be?"

"Because I left you for that life."

There wasn't a flicker of ambivalence in his eyes. "But we've resolved that."

"Oh, Jeff!" She wrapped her arms around him and held tightly. "I can't believe this! It's like being able to have everything! Us and my career and Bison City, too."

Noelle dealt both of them a sturdy kick. They laughed together, sharing the moment.

BAILEY AND JOSIE WENT SHOPPING the following afternoon, and Jeff met Matt for a drink at the Silver Horn Grill's lounge.

"Since when have you had time," Jeff asked as he took the stool beside his brother, "to wander off for a drink in the middle of the afternoon?"

"Since I heard about Bailey's award." Matt reached for his bourbon and Seven. "That's quite an accomplishment."

"Yes, it is."

"And you're going back to New York with her."

"Right."

Jeff knew what this careful sidestepping was building up to. He'd always resented the fact that Matt never missed a detail in the lives of his brothers and sister, and that he always seemed to understand how they would be affected by whatever happened.

"If you're about to ask me if I'm prepared to have to come back alone," he said, swirling the bourbon in his barrel glass, "I'm not."

Matt shook his head. "I was going to ask you if you realize just how much you've come to love each other."

Matt took a deep swig and felt its smooth heat all the way down to his stomach. "She says she's loved me since last April. But love isn't the deciding factor for her. She's had a lifetime of putting off what she wanted to do—and now she's won an award for being able to do it even by remote."

"Must be a powerful talent."

"Yeah."

"You have to have faith in what she feels for you. Half the skill in loving someone is letting yourself believe that you're loved in return." Matt sipped at his glass, then put it down on the bar. "As generally unlovable as you are, I can see why that's hard for you."

Jeff gave him a condemning look. "Thanks for your support."

"What's a brother for? The other half of loving is forgetting what it costs you."

"I know that."

"Then you're maybe considering having to live in New York for her?"

Jeff didn't look at him. He didn't want him to see how much he hated that possibility. He could live there if he had to, and he could live there happily if he had Bailey and their baby. But his heart lived in Bison City, Wyoming. He didn't want to run the ranch like Matt did, but he wanted to be able to go there when he felt like it, to walk around the place, to stop at the little cemetery where Samuel and Jocasta lay and imagine the man who'd dropped a fortune in gold to the bottom of the sea in order to take the woman he loved to safety.

He wanted to look out a window or step outside and see the snowcapped Bighorn Mountains.

"Yeah, I am."

"Good." Matt slapped him on the back and slipped off the stool. "Just wanted to make sure. Got to get back."

"You should direct all this mature wisdom toward yourself someday," Jeff said, turning on his stool to watch Matt pull up the collar of his sheepskin-lined jacket. "One day you're going to have to forget what it'll cost you to put the past away and start another family."

"I have a family," Matt countered.

Jeff nodded. "Yeah. And we'll all be relieved when you get your own so you'll leave us alone. But...thanks."

"You going to need a ride to the airport?"

"No, I'll just leave the car there."

"All right. Take care."

JEFF KNEW IT WAS COWARDLY, but he did his best not to think. As the plane circled above the sea of concrete as far as the eye could see, as the cab drove through miles of congestion on the street, on the sidewalk and absolutely everywhere the eye fell, even as he spotted familiar landmarks from the years he'd lived in Manhattan, he absorbed the sensory details but didn't think about them.

Though he would have had to be comatose not to see how they affected Bailey. He'd expected exuberance and excitement, but instead he noticed a deep-down happiness, a kind of internal radiance that had nothing to do with her pregnancy.

She was home.

That struck him like a sledgehammer right between the eyes.

What in the hell was he going to do about that?

Nothing for the moment. He was here as moral support and protection, and he was determined to provide both without thought to himself or his concerns.

The hotel suite was palatial and made The Way Station's offerings look humble. The room had high ceilings, gilt-trimmed moldings in what he guessed was a French style and opulent appointments everywhere you turned.

The bedroom was huge, the bed canopied in an old-rose-patterned fabric that matched the bedspread and drapes. The television and VCR were concealed in an armoire, and a thick white rug covered the floor.

A large fruit-and-chocolate basket stood on the ornate dresser. Bailey investigated and discovered that it was from Yvonne.

The view from the two floor-to-ceiling windows was of exclusive shops, fashionably dressed women and men in overcoats. Cars and taxicabs drove by, an occasional honk punctuating the quieter midafternoon hubbub.

Jeff remembered that the view from his apartment

had been similar, though several important blocks south.

He guessed that Bailey was exhausted, though she hadn't complained once of the crowded conditions on the plane, and the hurrying to make connections. They'd left Bison City the night before and stayed in Casper, then flown out this morning.

"How about a warm shower," he asked, turning toward her, "and a nap until din—" He stopped abruptly when she snapped a square of chocolate in half and popped one piece into his mouth while munching down on the other.

"No nap," she said around the chocolate, reaching to the bed where she'd tossed her jacket. "I have to find something to wear tomorrow night."

He wanted to protest that she could do that tomorrow, but the candy in his mouth and the fact that she already had the door open and was waiting for him would have made it futile.

She asked a cabbie to take them to the Motherhood Mart on Broadway. On the way she indicated points of interest to no one but her, but he was still fascinated by how much she'd learned about the city in such a short time. She'd been in New York less than a year and understood its basic layout and where to find what, while he'd been here eight years and, all things considered, had learned very little except what lay between work and home and his little corner of Long Island.

He knew that their attitudes had made the difference. She'd always wanted to be here. He'd come because he thought it was where he should be...and eventually had discovered that it wasn't.

He turned away from that thought and concentrated on her quest for the *big* black dress because, as she put it, "I'd never fit into a *little* one."

He sat behind her in an upholstered chair, sipping at a cup of coffee provided by a sympathetic clerk who'd helped her in and out of a dozen dresses. Bailey now wore a dress with thin, shoelace straps and a skirt that skimmed her knees. She looked at herself in horror, then turned to him.

"When did my arms get so huge?"

"Your arms are not huge," he assured her.

"I hate this."

"Then try something else on."

"No, I mean I hate trying to look stylish when I'm so enormous." The trip to the doctor's before they left had revealed a weight gain of three pounds, and she'd closed her eyes in self-loathing.

He rested his coffee in the pot of a palm next to his chair, then set their jackets on the chair and went to her. He turned her toward the triple mirror. He thought she looked beautiful from every angle.

"Look at yourself," he said, holding her by the shoulders. "Without thinking about the waistline you've lost, just look at your face."

With her mouth firmed in a frown that resisted his efforts to cheer her, she did as he asked.

She must be able to see what he saw. Her cheeks were pink and just full enough to make her look youthful and healthy. Her eyes were bright with the excitement of the trip and her own success, and her hair, done by Josie's hairdresser just before they'd left Bison City, was a riot of blond curls.

She finally allowed herself a hesitant smile.

"Now," he said, leaning over her to whisper into her ear as he rubbed a hand over her stomach, "you look like you've swallowed a globe because you have my whole world in there, and I don't just mean the baby. I mean that you have all of me, too, everything I want for us. And I'm telling you it's no small thing."

He'd hoped to watch her smile widen, but instead her face softened and she looked at his reflection with all the love he'd ever hoped to see in her eyes.

The clerk smiled at them as she handed Bailey a hanger with a long swath of something black and floaty hanging from it. "This will do it. Try it."

Bailey turned in his arms to pull his face down to her and kissed him with a fervor that made even the clerk blush. Then she went off to try on the dress.

Jeff went back to his chair and congratulated himself on almost understanding her.

The dress was perfect. It was calf length with layers of black tissue-thin fabric that fell from just beneath her breasts. The neckline was low with more layers of the fabric giving it a shawl-like effect.

Bailey did a turn that was all grace despite the advanced pregnancy. "What do you think? With black stockings and black shoes?"

"It's beautiful," he said. "You're beautiful. But you're telling me we have to go shopping for shoes?"

"No, I have some."

"Then it's perfect."

"No dressy coat, though."

"Hold on," the clerk said. "I have just the thing." She took off and was back in a moment with a black cape, its hood lined in bright pink. She put the hood up on Bailey's head and Bailey smiled at Jeff in question.

She looked like a woman some fictional, love-starved hero might find on the moors one stormy night.

"Also perfect," he said and went to pay the bill while she changed.

YVONNE PICKED UP Bailey and Jeff in a limousine that night and took them to Le Cirque for dinner.

Bailey couldn't remember ever being this happy. Yvonne was totally taken with Jeff, and he seemed to be enjoying her stories of mischievous child models, life in the fashion industry and Bailey's introduction to it by phone and fax.

"Her design teacher in college had been a friend of mine for ages," Yvonne told Jeff, "and I interviewed Bailey for an apprentice position a week after she graduated. She explained to me that her mother was ill, and she had to go home, but she asked if she could fax me designs.

"I didn't think that would work, but she made it work! Then she came to New York when she was able and produced a line of clothes that I'm sure will win her the award again next year."

Bailey rolled her eyes over the profuse praise. "You make me sound like some Coco Chanel for children." She covered Yvonne's hand when the woman would have gone on again. "Tell me about your love life, Yvonne." She grinned at Jeff. "It's very exciting. She has young men on the string, old men, rich men, royalty…"

Yvonne patted an elegant silver cap of hair. "When you can't get serious about one," she said philosophically, "you may as well enjoy the variety nature has to offer."

"So, who's your current swain?"

Yvonne blushed. "I've been seeing Ricardo Montenegro."

"No!" In an aside to Jeff, Bailey explained, "He designs men's casual clothes. Ralph Lauren with a Latin flair. Oh, Yvonne! Is he as dreamy as he looks—as his clothes look?"

"Every bit."

"Are we going to get to meet him?"

Yvonne shook her head regretfully. "He's in Havana on business until after Christmas."

"Wow. I'd love to have business in Havana."

"They're not giving you awards in Havana, sweetie. You have business here."

Bailey turned to Jeff with a smile over Yvonne's remark and caught a watchful and slightly sad look in his eyes. It brought a frown to her face and a sharpening of her attention. What was he thinking?

Several upsetting possibilities occurred to her, but she was forced to mentally push them aside when Yvonne leaned toward her and said with a smile, "I have a proposition for you, Bailey."

Bailey dragged her focus back to Yvonne. "Yes?"

"Yes." She shifted in her chair, folded her napkin and put it aside. "I'm planning to split the line into two separate entities—casual and dressy. I'd like to put you in charge of the casual."

Bailey heard the words but couldn't quite believe them.

"You'd have free rein because I trust you so completely, but I would like to be kept apprised of what you're doing. I know you wanted to start your own line eventually, but this would be a good way to segue into that. You'd have to take care of everything, see what it's like to run a line in its entirety. And you'd be funded by me, of course. I assure you that's much easier than having to back yourself. What do you say?"

Bailey was speechless. She turned to Jeff in complete astonishment, and though he was smiling, she saw the same look in his eyes she'd seen before. It almost snapped her out of the thrill of having been offered to run one half of a prestigious design house.

"Oh. One more thing," Yvonne added. "There is a hitch. You'd have to do it here in New York."

Bailey felt her excitement sputter. "Why?"

"Because we'd have to coordinate plans, shows, and with you being in charge of casual wear, you'll have to deal with seamstresses, suppliers, models, manufacturers—more tasks than you could handle from the wilds of Wyoming." She smiled at Jeff. "No offense intended, Jeff."

He shook his head. "None taken."

Bailey allowed herself one more moment of having the perfect job placed in her lap, then accepted—with more peaceful resignation that she'd thought herself capable of—that fate had snatched it away again with the details.

"Our home's in Bison City, Yvonne," she said. "I don't think—"

"*I* think," Jeff interrupted quietly, "that you

should think about it.'' He looked at Yvonne. ''Can she tell you tomorrow night at the dinner?''

Yvonne made a face. ''Well, I'd sleep much better tonight if I knew now, but okay. Bailey, sweetie, I'm offering you everything you've wanted. An award is important but it doesn't make your career. Producing winning designs year after year does that, and I can help you make that happen. Think about it. How hard is it to move a household, anyway?''

Moving a household would be no problem. Moving a McIntyre would be something else again.

Why did Jeff want her to think about it? She didn't like that look in his eyes, either.

''Okay,'' she told Yvonne with a smile she didn't feel. ''We'll talk about it again tomorrow night.''

BAILEY WALKED from the suite's bathroom to the bed in a pink-and-white-striped flannel nightgown that she thought made her look a little like an animated cabana. She rubbed absently at her side as she climbed in under the covers.

Jeff, in boxers and white T-shirt, flipped off the light and went to join her. She hadn't said a word about Yvonne's offer. Jeff was sure she wanted to, but was reluctant to confront his opposition.

He wrapped an arm around Bailey, his hand resting comfortably on Noelle, and broached the subject. ''Are you excited about Yvonne's proposition?'' he asked.

He felt her tense and kissed her hair, determined to stop her from refusing what she wanted most in all the world.

"Of course I'm excited," she said. "It's a wonderful opportunity."

He squeezed her a little tighter. "Then I think you should take it. It would be criminal to pass up a chance you've worked so hard for under such difficult circumstances." He felt guilty that he'd taken her away from the place that put that I'm-home smile on her face and that seemed to appreciate her skill and flair with children's clothes.

She was silent for a long moment, her body under his hand very still and tense. "I'm thinking about it," she said in a small voice.

"That's good," he said. He ran a hand up her side and felt the little knot between her ribs that was probably Noelle's toes. He began to rub, imagining the position of the tiny body probably desperate for moving room in her mother's confining womb.

"What about Noelle?" she asked, her voice a little high in the darkness. "I mean, if I take the job."

"It's not the place I'd choose to raise a child," he replied, "but they're adaptable, I understand."

"Yes. That's what I hear."

"Then she'll be fine."

"Yes."

Bailey felt the long, uncontrolled drop into darkness. She'd thought Jeff was dealing with a dilemma all evening. So that was it. He'd been preparing to say goodbye.

No. That couldn't be. As his hand rubbed gently up and down her side in what had become their nightly ritual, she remembered standing in front of the mirror at the Motherhood Mart that very afternoon and looking into the eyes of a man who loved her.

What was going on here? How could he profess to love her one moment—to tell her that she carried his entire world and all he hoped for—then be willing to leave her in New York the next?

"You're…willing to let me stay here?" she asked outright.

"No," he replied, planting a kiss in her ear. She felt a rush of relief. "Noelle has to be born in Bison City. Your doctor's there, the folks and the family will be there. I'm sure Yvonne won't expect you to take the job until you've had the baby."

She plunged into the hole a second time. He wasn't going to leave her here, but he was going to let her come back after Noelle was born. To New York. By herself. Two thousand miles away from him.

But he'd accepted her proposal. She was wearing his ring.

"Jeff, I don't…" She started to turn onto her back to ask him what had happened to change his mind when a pain ripped across her abdomen with a force that stole her breath. She put a hand to it and grimaced. "Ah!"

"What?" Jeff propped himself up on an elbow and put a hand to hers on the mound of her belly. His eyes were dark with concern. "What's the matter?"

Frightened, she lay still, waiting for a second pain or an echo of the first one, but it was gone as quickly as it had come.

"Just a pain," she said, everything feeling normal again. Noelle moved, that, too, feeling very normal.

"What do you mean? What kind of pain? A contraction?"

"I'm not sure," she replied honestly. "Maybe. But it's too soon. I don't know what it was. But it's gone."

"Well…early contractions are pretty far apart, aren't they?" He glanced at his watch, then returned his attention to her, caressing Noelle. "You think you've started labor?"

She concentrated on focusing on the baby, on ignoring Jeff's sudden change in attitude about letting her come back to New York. Maybe anxiety had caused the pain. "No, I don't think so. My water hasn't broken." She drew a deep breath and felt nothing unusual. "Everything seems to be okay."

Noelle kicked again, right under his hand. "She seems to be all right," he said.

"Yeah. Lie down, Jeff. I think I'm fine."

He wrapped her in his arms and held her close. "I'll watch you for a while. One more pain and I'm calling someone." He held her close to his shoulder, his other hand stroking gently over her hair. "You just relax. Try to sleep."

The soothing touch of his hand helped to push aside everything about tonight that confused her, and it encouraged her to close her eyes and drift off to sleep, secure in the knowledge that if she did have a second pain, he'd probably know about it before she did.

HE WAS LEANING OVER HER when she awoke. He wore brown cords and a white sweater with a brown horizontal pattern. She put her fingertips to it, her worries of the night before still there, still confusing.

"I haven't seen you wear this," she said, liking the way the pattern exaggerated his broad shoulders.

He smiled gently. "Josie gave it to me for a birthday. I put it away and forgot I had it. It seemed like something to wear in the big city." His eyes grew serious. "How do you feel this morning? Once you fell asleep you didn't even move."

She felt wonderful—physically, at least. "I don't know what that was, but I feel great."

"Well, that's a relief." He leaned forward to kiss her cheek. "You scared me."

"Me, too," she admitted. "I'm starving. Have you seen the room service menu? I'd love to just lie here propped up against the pillows and eat something huge and disgustingly rich in cholesterol."

He went to the dresser where the menu lay and brought it back to the bed. He sat down beside her again and perused it. "Ah. This is it. The farmer's omelette with bacon, sausage, ham and cheese. With hash browns and toast or pancakes?"

"Hash browns. Whole wheat toast."

He grinned. "On a health kick, huh?" He reached for the phone on his side of the bed and placed the order.

They watched a morning news show, then delved into a basket of goodies his family had sent and polished off breakfast with chocolate balls from Yvonne's basket.

"This is so wonderfully decadent," Bailey said,

stretching her arms up over her head. "But I suppose I should get up and do something constructive."

"Why?" he challenged. He sat beside her atop the coverlet in his stocking feet. "You're being feted as a star tonight. The day is yours to indulge yourself in whatever way you want."

"Did you ever take a carriage ride in Central Park while you were here?" she asked.

"No. Did you?"

"No, but I always wanted to. Shall we do that today?"

"Sounds good to me."

Looking into his smiling eyes, she was a breath away from bringing up her return to New York, but a late-fall sun was streaming through the window, the day had begun so beautifully, and it was going to end with her receiving an award from her peers. She didn't want to do anything to ruin the atmosphere.

"I can be ready in half an hour," she promised.

"I'll believe that when I see it."

Chapter Thirteen

They returned to the hotel room in the middle of the afternoon, but only because Jeff insisted. "You have to get some rest if you're going to dazzle everyone tonight."

Bailey leaned lazily against him as he unlocked the door. "I could ride in a carriage all the time. Whoever invented cars, anyway? Sitting close together under a blanket with the clip-clop of the horse's hooves and the rocking of the carriage is so much more romantic than doing seventy on the freeway with the CD player blaring."

"That's true." He held the door open for her.

"I'll bet that's how Samuel and Jocasta got places." She tossed her purse and coat on a chair and went toward the basket his family had sent.

"I'm sure it was." He manacled her wrist in his and withdrew it from the basket. "Bailey, you're going to be sick. You had a gyro for lunch, cheesecake for dessert and a pretzel slathered in mustard in the middle of the afternoon. And I'm sure we're in for a big dinner tonight."

She showed him what she'd snagged from the basket and it wasn't food at all. It was the small bottle of massage oil. Probably Josie's contribution. He looked into Bailey's eyes and saw trouble there.

Not that he wasn't used to dealing with trouble since he'd first met her. He'd squired her around the city today and watched her blossom amidst the sights and sounds of this place he'd sworn he'd never return to again. But she'd made mincemeat of his future. And she was making his present pretty difficult, too.

She slipped her free hand under the hem of his sweater, her fingertips soft against the flesh of his stomach, his rib cage. "This will help us both relax."

"I don't think that's intended to help you relax," he said.

"That's the point. We're in the big city. Big things happen here." She lifted his sweater higher and put her lips to his chest.

And that was all it took to decimate his resolve. She should be resting, but damned if he could muster any will to turn her from her determination to seduce him. In fact, he carried her to the bed and cheerfully did all he could to assist her in achieving her goal.

BAILEY PUT PEARL studs in her ears and stood back from the cheval mirror in the bedroom to assess her appearance. She'd awakened from the nap she and Jeff had finally taken after their lovemaking to find a note on his pillow that said he'd gone down to the lobby and would be back in time to escort her downstairs. Yvonne and her chauffeur would be picking them up at seven.

She expelled a little sigh as she studied the beautiful lines of her dress, the well-loved look on her face, and realized that for the first time in months she felt attractive. Still enormous, she thought with a laugh, but attractive.

And she could not believe that Jeff could have made love to her the way he did this afternoon and still plan to send her and Noelle back here after the baby was born. He was doing this because he was convinced it was what *she* wanted. She had to make clear to him that living here was no longer her life's dream. While she'd have loved designing and running Yvonne's casual line, nothing in the world was more important to her now than Jeff and their daughter and Jeff's family. She now thought of them as hers, too.

She was about to reach for her coat when the telephone rang. Expecting it to be Jeff, telling her he was on his way up, she was surprised to hear a strange man's voice.

"Bailey Dutton?" he asked.

"Yes," she replied.

"I'm Ira Binford with Island Properties. I've found you a rent-controlled apartment on the Upper East Side that you're going to love. Jeff told me if I found anything before you left that you'd want to look at it. I understand you have big doings tonight, but what about if I pick you up at 9:00 a.m. tomorrow and take you there?"

Holding the phone to her ear, she stared at her reflection in stupefaction. Jeff was already finding her an apartment?

"Mr. Binford," she said firmly, "Jeff was mistaken about my wanting to live here."

"But, he—"

"Whatever he told you doesn't apply. You can stop looking for an apartment for me. I'm not coming back. But thank you for your efforts. Good night."

"But—"

She hung up, more than a little annoyed that she was still enraptured by the love she and Jeff had found and expressed so perfectly only hours ago— and he was out finding her a place to live without him!

Unwilling to wait another moment to straighten this out with him, she put on her cape, let the hood fall back and transferred the few things she'd need from her purse to her pockets. Then she got on an elevator.

On the bottom floor she rounded the corner of the desk to the columned lobby with its overstuffed furnishings in gold and white and spotted Jeff at the far end. She raised her hand to get his attention, then quickly lowered it when she saw that he wasn't alone.

Miranda Parker smiled up at him in a red silk Mandarin-style sheath split up the side to the middle of her thigh. Every sleek line of her and every neat and slender curve was revealed by the fabric.

Bailey experienced a violent surge of jealousy— both for that body and for the fact that Jeff now had his hands on it at her waist. Miranda reached up to wrap her arms around his neck and hold him for a moment, then she handed him a small gift-wrapped box topped with a silver bow.

Jealousy, fury and grief rioted inside her. It felt like a martial arts competition going on in her chest, and she put an instinctive hand to Noelle to protect her.

Then Miranda hurried through the hotel's double glass doors just as a liveried chauffeur walked in and headed for the desk. Jeff intercepted him, swept his hand toward the chairs, apparently inviting him to sit, then turned toward the elevators, presumably to go upstairs to get Bailey.

He spotted her near the desk and came to her, the little box still in his hand. "I knew you'd get hungry and impatient," he teased with a grin. He tried to hand her the box. "This is—"

She pushed it away. "I saw her give it to you." Her heart was broken, and she swore she could feel it bleeding. But for the moment at least she was more angry than sad. She'd let herself be bullied into leaving New York for Bison City by his threats of filing for custody of Noelle, then, despite that, she'd allowed him to convince her that he loved her and wanted to build his life with her. "And Ira Binford called about an apartment. I didn't understand at first why you were so anxious to unload us."

"What?" His smile changed to a look of confusion.

"I thought you were motivated by some selfless desire to give me what you thought I wanted."

He shifted his weight, his brain clearly working to try to keep up with her. "I'm not following you, Bailey," he said.

She tied the frog fastener at the neckline of her coat and angled her chin. "And I'm not following you anymore, Jeff. I'm going back to Bison City with you because I owe the Millennium Baby project my support. Then you and I are carving out a legal agreement for custody of Noelle, then I'm out of your life.'' She tried to pull off her ring, intending to terminate this conversation with the return of it, but her hands were swollen and it wouldn't come off.

Embarrassed and even more angry, she held up her left hand and pointed to it. ''The minute I can get this thing off, you're getting it back.'' She tried to stride past him toward the doors, but he caught her arm.

''What are you talking about?'' he demanded.

''Lies!'' she replied. ''Deception! Little honeys on the side!''

''What?''

''Darlings!'' Yvonne bustled into the lobby, now filled with guests and staff staring at them. She wore silver lamé and looked strikingly handsome when she paused for a moment and looked around her in surprise at the tableau—Jeff and Bailey fuming at each other, everyone watching. Then she apparently decided there wasn't time to worry about that. ''We're going to be late if we don't leave right this minute. Are you ready?''

Bailey hooked an arm in hers. ''Let's go,'' she said.

Jeff wasn't entirely sure what had happened, but guessed from Bailey's remark about ''honeys on the side'' that she'd seen Miranda hug him. Granted, Bailey was emotionally unpredictable because of her condition, but this was more than that. Though what, precisely, he didn't know.

He just knew they were having it out the moment this interminable evening was over. And that couldn't come soon enough. Bailey directed all her conversation at Yvonne and never turned to him once, despite Yvonne's efforts to draw him into the conversation.

Bailey kept her distance from him through a cocktail party where he was befriended by an older man whose wife was here in some capacity, abandoning him also. But he was a baseball fanatic, and Jeff's game was football. He listened patiently, however, just for something to do.

A dinner of something very nouvelle cuisine, with small portions and dramatic swirls of sauces and garnish, felt like an appetizer. That was followed by a parade of beautiful children modeling the critical favorites of the award-winning lines.

Then the awards were presented. Bailey was the fourth name announced, and she earned enthusiastic applause. The bloom he'd seen on her yesterday was gone, replaced by a pale fragility accentuated by the ruffles around her shoulders and the dark and delicate fabric.

His anger diminished a little in the face of the power of whatever had caused this change in her. Just a few days ago she'd asked him to marry her, and now she looked as though she hadn't a friend in the world, much less a lover.

She returned to the table looking as though accepting the award had wilted her temper, and by the time the program was over, all that was left in her porcelain face was a very visible misery.

That did it for him. While everyone stood around talking and laughing, he got her coat, then caught her hand. She looked into his eyes without expression, as though he was a complete stranger, and tried to pull away. But he held on.

"We're going back to the hotel," he said.

Yvonne, within earshot, came to frown at them. "But I don't have her answer yet. She promised we'd talk after the awards. And Miranda Parker wanted to see you."

"She's already seen him, thanks," Bailey said with a glare in his direction. "Why don't we talk over breakfast, Yvonne. In the hotel dining room?"

Yvonne looked doubtful. "Is something wrong? You two haven't been yourselves all evening."

"This *is* us," Bailey said. "Good night, Yvonne."

JEFF DIDN'T SAY A WORD in the cab. He sat stiffly beside Bailey like a chunk of Mount Rushmore come to New York.

They marched across the lobby side by side. Actually, he marched and she was forced to run to keep up because he had a tight grip on her hand.

They said nothing in the elevator, though they occupied the car alone, but the moment he closed the door to their suite behind him, it was as though fire had burned up a fuse and something very large and very deadly exploded.

"What in the hell is wrong with you?" he demanded, yanking off his jacket. "You have been a little monster all evening, and please don't tell me it's because you saw Miranda put her arms around me in the lobby!"

The release of his temper sparked hers into full display. "Did you really think I wouldn't object to that? You leave me in the bed where you just made love to me for a clandestine meeting in the lobby with your former lover who gives you a gift and you're surprised that I'm upset?''

''We *were* lovers,'' he said, lowering his voice though his eyes maintained their turbulent intensity, ''but that was a long time ago.''

''Then what is she doing here right where you happen to be staying?''

He'd stormed away from her when they'd entered the room, but now he came back to stop within inches of her. ''Because she's a reporter who was sent here to do a story on you—their regional celebrity and the star of tonight's festivities. I can't believe you thought she'd followed *me*. Or that I'd arranged to have you in this room and her in another. Is that what you thought?''

The horrified blush that rose to the roots of her hair was his answer.

He shook his head at her. ''And I have no idea how you can call a meeting 'clandestine' when it takes place in a hotel lobby filled with people, and as for the gift...'' He went to the bed where his jacket lay, found the left pocket and withdrew the little box. ''It was for both of us.'' He handed it to her.

She folded her arms, unwilling to take it, a little icy niggle of dread inching along her spine. ''What do you mean, both of us?''

''How complicated a concept is *both of us?*'' He took her hand and slapped the box into it. ''But what am I thinking? The way you acted tonight, there's no way you've ever thought of you and me as an entity. Open it.''

She tried to give it back. "You open it."

"Open it," he repeated in a voice she'd never heard before and didn't like at all.

Bailey tore the paper off the box, lifted the lid and found a small square card with a baby rattle on it. In a graceful hand in lavender ink, it said, "Jeff and Bailey—Congratulations on your parenthood! I wish I was brave enough. Love, Randy."

In the box was a tiny pair of yellow crocheted booties.

"She came to the hotel to interview you before the dinner tonight," he said, "but you were still sleeping, so I told her you'd talk to her after the awards. That's why Yvonne said she wanted to see us—not to see me, but to see you."

Tears crowded her throat. She felt small and stupid and frankly horrified, but she still didn't think she had to bear all the blame for her confusion about Miranda.

"Well, when you changed your mind about our staying together," she said, her voice high and raspy, "I couldn't figure out why until I saw her. Then…it all came together."

"Well, it may have come together," he said loudly, "but it didn't *fit*. I have no romantic involvement with her. And what do you mean about changing my mind?"

She spread her arms impatiently. "You said I belonged here and you were going to send me back! You got a Realtor to find me an apartment!"

For a moment he stared at her as though she'd spoken those words in Martian. Then something changed in his eyes and he closed them and shook his head again.

"Bailey Dutton," he said, keeping his distance, "you amaze me. Where have you been during all the time we've spent together? Where the hell were you this afternoon when I made love to you?"

Now she was the one who didn't understand.

"Worried about your independence, I imagine," he said, answering his own question. "So afraid that our relationship would take something from you rather than give you anything that you've never noticed how much I love you."

"You were finding me an apartment!" she shouted at him. "Two thousand miles away from you!"

"Did you really think that I was going to send you here *alone?*" he roared back at her. "That the apartment was just for you and not for both of us? For the three of us?"

She was starting to shake. Little tremors deep inside her were working their way to the surface. "You...were coming?" she asked, her voice barely there.

"I was going to be married to you. I think that's usually how that works. You live in the same place."

"But you hate New York."

"Yes, I do," he admitted without a moment's thought. "But you love it here and you have that offer from Yvonne, and I have to be with you."

She had difficulty grasping that. The truth was so outrageous she couldn't quite believe it. "You were coming *with* me?" she asked again.

He drew a breath for patience. "Yes. I was coming

with you. I saw your expression change the moment we got off the plane. You looked as though you'd come home. So I planned to leave mine in order for you to have yours.''

She burst into tears and sank onto the edge of the bed.

Jeff knew he had to let go of his anger and exasperation if he was going to get through to her. He was apparently doing something wrong. Explaining to her that they were moving to New York so she could take the job should have made her happy rather than driven her to tears.

He hitched up a pants leg and knelt on one knee in front of her. ''I don't understand why you're still upset,'' he said candidly. ''I'm trying to give you want you want.''

She dropped her hands and opened her mouth to answer, but a sharp cry came to her lips instead. A pain like the one she'd had last night tore across her abdomen, causing her to double over. And it persisted.

''What?'' Jeff demanded, leaning down to try to look into her face. ''Another pain?''

She nodded, fear for the baby quickening her heartbeat. ''And it's not…going away.''

But Jeff was already on the phone. In five minutes she was in an ambulance on her way to New York Hospital's emergency room, and in ten more a young OB-GYN had her attached to monitors and was doing tests. Bailey admitted in some embarrassment that the pain was gone and she felt considerably better.

''I think it's just Braxton Hicks contractions,'' he

said with a smile. "It isn't labor, just your body sort of getting ready for it. It hurts a lot, but it doesn't really accomplish anything."

Like all my rantings about freedom, she thought, feeling just a little drowsy. They hurt a lot and accomplished nothing because true freedom wasn't an absence of responsibility, it was just an internal ease about accepting it. She'd only understood that now that she'd been willing to give up what she wanted for Jeff's sake, just as he'd been prepared to do for her.

"Can I see my fiancé?" she asked, suddenly desperate to feel his hand in hers.

"Sure. I'm going to see if your tests are back yet and send him in here."

In a moment Jeff pushed aside the curtain surrounding her bed, and she reached both arms up to him, wanting nothing else in all the world but to be in his.

He leaned over her, his hands trembling around her. "Are you all right?" he asked, his voice strained. "What did he say?"

She explained about the phoney contractions. "He thinks that's all it is, but he's gone to see if my tests are back."

He pulled up a small stool nearby and sat beside her. But he had to do it one-handed because she wouldn't let go of him.

"Jeff, I don't want to live in New York," she said, as though the past traumatic half hour hadn't interrupted their argument. "If I...if I looked as though I'd come home, it was because I'd brought you home with me. You. You're home to me. When I got off the plane, I thought it was great that…that we got to be here together because I do love it here, but it's not where I want to be anymore.''

Jeff was hearing the words, but they weren't computing with what he thought he knew to be true. ''Where,'' he asked, ''do you want to be?''

She ground his hand in hers. ''In Bison City with Josie and Annie and your family and your staff and everyone else that now makes up my life.''

''But the job—''

''I was going to turn it down and go home with you.''

''But I was moving us back here so you could take it.''

''I don't want to take it if I have to stay here. I'll just work on my own line from home. God, Jeff, I'm so sorry about tonight, but one minute I was so happy knowing we were in love, then you were telling me to take the job, and the Realtor was calling, and I thought—''

''It's all right. Never mind.'' He kissed her hand.

The only thing that would make him happier at this moment was the confirmation that the doctor was right and there was nothing wrong with Bailey but false labor.

He got it an instant later when the doctor reappeared with a clean bill of health for Bailey and Noelle. ''We love scary things that turn out to be nothing. You got a name for this little guy?''

Bailey sat up, Jeff standing by the bed to help her. ''Girl, you mean,'' she said. ''Yes, we do. Noelle.''

The doctor raised an eyebrow. ''You said when

you had your first ultrasound, they told you the sex of your baby.''

She nodded. "Yes. A girl." Then she glanced at Jeff and back to the doctor. "Why? Was that wrong?"

He held up the ultrasound they'd just taken, tracing the outline of the definitive feature with his pen. "Very," he said.

Jeff barked a surprised laugh. "You're right. That is not a girl." He wrapped his arms around Bailey, who looked completely baffled.

"Happens sometimes," the doctor explained with a grin. "Clues can be concealed, depending upon the position of a leg or a hand. Try to relax. I'd say you've got a good month to go."

Bailey blinked and focused on the doctor. "My due date is Christmas Day."

The doctor shrugged. "Could happen, but my guess is you'll go a little longer. You haven't dropped, and first-time mothers usually drop two to four weeks before delivery. The important thing is he's strong and perfect and he'll just get more so in the next month. I'm pretty good at calling these." He grinned again. "But you're going to need another name."

In the cab back to the hotel just before one in the morning, Bailey tried to adjust to the changes that had taken place in her life in the past three hours. Jeff loved her, after all, she was going home to Bison City, and she was carrying a son!

Wrapped in Jeff's arms in a corner of the back seat, she watched the neon lights of Broadway go by and heaved a deep sigh. She had everything. Bailey

Dutton, who'd thought her happiness lay in the pursuit of her dreams, had just learned that you could wake up and find yourself in the middle of one—and that it could be better than anything you could plan or conjure.

Jeff tightened his grip on her. "Don't be disappointed. We'll have a girl next time."

She snuggled closer and felt a laugh bubble up. It came from deep inside and seemed significant of her new lightness of being. She laughed again at the notion of her rotund body and lightness in the same thought.

"I'm not disappointed." She tipped her head back to look into Jeff's face. "I've loved this baby since I first suspected I was pregnant. Even when I knew how much my life would change, I wanted her—him—so much. And some of that was because he was part of you, and I thought then that I couldn't have you. But here we are." She reached up to kiss him. "I'm not dreaming this, am I? You do want me and the baby as much as we want you?"

He returned the kiss. "Bailey, I was going to live in New York for you. Don't ever doubt how much I love you and little what's-his-name."

"I don't like the name Noel as much as I liked Noelle," she said. "Let's name him after you."

He shook his head. "He should have his own identity. But what if we name him for his uncles?"

"You mean...Mathew Alexander Justin McIntyre?"

He repeated it slowly, then nodded. "Yeah. I like it. Do you?"

"I do. But what am I going to do with all the pink

fabric I bought for us? Annie and Josie are having boys, too.''

He laughed softly and squeezed her to him. ''We have the blue crocheted afghan Matt's wife Julie made for me for Christmas. Little Matt can use that. Maybe Elizabeth will have a girl.''

Suddenly tired, Bailey kissed his throat, then said on a yawn, ''If not, we'll just save it for another time.''

YVONNE LISTENED with a frown while Bailey explained over breakfast that it was impossible for her to stay in New York even though her husband was willing, and that she would have to turn down the generous offer.

''But you've always wanted to be here,'' Yvonne protested. ''And if Jeff's willing, I don't see…''

Bailey smiled, feeling serene. ''My life's in Wyoming now, with the best people in the whole world. I'm sorry, Yvonne.''

Yvonne expelled a gusty breath. ''Well, I'm sorry, too, because I wasn't anxious to have to deal with you by phone and fax again, but it seems that's what I'm going to have to do, after all. At least until you start your own design company and we become competitors. You're hired, anyway, and I'll expect some brilliant work as soon as that baby is born!''

Bailey recounted that conversation to Josie, Annie, Elizabeth and all the other women at Bailey's baby shower in The Way Station's dining room. Leon had gone all out with outrageous desserts and booties with silk flowers in them at every place.

Elizabeth leaned her chin in her hand and smiled

across the long table at Bailey. "Well, if you haven't turned out to be the most disgustingly perfect happy ending I've ever seen. And the best part is that it isn't ending at all, it's just beginning."

"Well, that's true of most of us," Josie said, looking around the table. A good percentage of the women there were pregnant. "Babies kind of renew a mother's life, too, don't they? And everyone nearby is energized by the glow."

Elizabeth grinned. "I'd like to be energized by the right man."

Jeff suddenly appeared in the dining room, a cordless phone in hand, Leon hovering beside him, his eyes wide. Jeff made his way to Bailey.

She started to get to her feet, alarm filling her. "Is something wrong?"

He smiled and pushed her gently back into her chair. "Not at all. In fact, quite the opposite." He glanced up and down the table at the other women. "Good afternoon, ladies."

"Who is it?" Bailey whispered.

He opened his mouth to reply, then seemed to change his mind. "Just answer it." He pushed the talk button for her.

She put the phone to her ear and said cautiously, "Hello?"

She heard a pleasant female voice she didn't recognize, then the words "…with the *Oprah* show." "Oprah?" she breathed. There were gasps and wide eyes up and down the table. Everyone leaned toward her.

"We'd like you and several of your ladies to appear on the show. Josie Moore, who started the con-

test, and Annie Thatcher. Then we understand there's
a doctor you've all been seeing who is pregnant herself and a contender for mother of the Millennium
Baby?''

''That's Elizabeth Lee,'' Bailey said.

Elizabeth's eyebrows went up, then down in a suspicious frown.

The caller began to give Bailey details about when
Oprah would like them to appear. Bailey made a
writing motion to Jeff, who handed her a pen and
the back of a business card. She wrote down the per-
tinent information, the woman said she would be in
touch again and was looking forward to meeting her.
Bailey hung up the phone in a state of stupefaction.

A banquet table was surrounded by women waiting for the details. Jeff and Leon stood by quietly.

She leaned back in her chair and said in utter disbelief, ''Josie, Annie and Elizabeth and I are going
to be on the *Oprah* show for the Millennium Baby
Contest!''

Josie squealed, then snatched the phone to call Justin. Annie simply stared, and Elizabeth looked horrified. ''Why *me?*''

''They heard that you're the doctor who's been
taking care of all of us, and since you're pregnant
yourself, I guess that's newsy stuff.''

''I can't go on television!''

Warming to the idea and what it could mean for
the hospital, Bailey dismissed her concern with a
shake of her head. ''Of course you can. I've done it.
It's a cinch.'' At Jeff's raised eyebrow, she added
candidly, ''Okay, not quite a cinch. It was only local
television, and I was scared spitless the whole time,

but if you want a machine to do ultrasounds, we have to do this.''

Elizabeth was suddenly interested. ''You can buy a machine? You're kidding!''

''I'm not. I'll show you the contest's bank account. An appearance on *Oprah* and we can probably start our own cloning operation.''

Leon made a scornful sound. ''I'm sure you'll get flak from the men of Bison City who prefer the old method of reproduction.''

''They have my vote,'' Jeff said.

JEFF, SONNY AND MAUREEN helped Bailey carry her shower gifts up to the suite after the guests left to pass on the exciting news. Gifts were piled on and around the bed in the room Bailey had used when she'd first arrived. That seemed an eternity ago.

Maureen and Sonny headed for the door hand in hand.

Jeff sent Bailey a questioning look that she responded to with an I-don't-know shrug of her shoulders.

Sonny caught the gesture. ''We're going to the movies tonight,'' he said. ''I've watched you two take control of a dicey situation and decided that the least I could do was take control of a lonely one.'' He smiled adoringly at Maureen, who blushed. ''I took Maureen to lunch, she invited me to spend Thanksgiving with her and her children, and we've been seeing each other ever since.'' He looked at Jeff in sudden concern. ''You don't have any rules against fraternizing, do you?''

Jeff laughed. ''Actually, I believe in it. Just be

discreet on the job. We now have an elevator for rendezvous.''

When Jeff closed the door behind them, Bailey sat among her treasures and turned the key on a musical lamb that had been a gift from Elizabeth. It played Brahms's ''Lullaby.'' She cleared a space for Jeff as he returned, her eyes soft but grave. ''Thank you for caring,'' she said as the gentle tune played accompaniment. ''Even when I tried so hard not to.''

He wrapped an arm around her, basking in the love in her eyes. ''I made love to you, Bailey. I knew what you felt. And I knew you'd have to deal with it eventually. Thank you for not being turned off by my tendency to make everyone's decisions for them.'' He laughed in self-deprecation. ''It comes from a lifetime of fighting Matt for the right.''

She put her free hand to his face, the love also in her touch. ''It's all right. You dropped your gold to save me.''

He didn't quite get that. He turned his lips into her palm and kissed it. ''Pardon me?''

''You would have moved to New York,'' she explained, ''because you thought I had to be there to be happy. That's like Samuel dropping his gold to get Jocasta to safety.''

''You're mine,'' he said, pulling her closer, loving the feel of her swollen belly against him. ''Keeping you safe is my job.''

She wrapped her arms and leaned into him. ''Then just keep me right here,'' she said.

Epilogue

December 31, 11:08 p.m.

"Bailey, for heaven's sake." Jeff stood beside the bed in which she'd lain in labor for the last nine hours and provided her handhold on sanity while she breathed her way through another interminable contraction. "Let the baby come!"

She waited the eternity it took for the pain to pass, then breathed heavily while he mopped her face with a washcloth. "Jeff, do you really think I'd want to continue this labor indefinitely if this baby had any intention of coming out?"

He glanced at the clock. "You're trying to make it to midnight," he accused. "I know you are."

Outside, horns were honking as someone held a drive-by New Year's celebration a little early.

"I'm just trying to make it," she corrected breathlessly, "to the birth."

"Good." He leaned over her earnestly. He'd been a stalwart support, but she could see that the grisly third stage of labor was getting to him as much as it was getting to her. "Because if you're trying to hold out for gifts or the fame of having the Millennium Baby, I'm here to tell you this baby is the most special thing in the world to me next to you no matter what time he's born, so let's just do it, okay?''

She kissed the hand she held, amazed that in the middle of the most excruciating pain she'd ever known, she could be this happy.

''Don't give out on me now,'' she said. ''This is the best part. Mathew Alexander Justin McIntyre is about to make his appearance. He just might not be ready till midnight. I'm not in control of this, Jeff. And you aren't either. *He* is. So try to relax. How's Annie doing?'' She'd been admitted just before Bailey. Josie had come in right after.

A quick rap on the door was followed by Matt's head peering around it. ''How's it going in here?''

''Nothing new to report,'' Jeff replied. ''Any babies yet?''

''Nope.'' He nodded toward Bailey. ''She's holding out to have the Millennium Baby, too, isn't she? I swear that's what they're all doing.''

Jeff smiled for the first time in hours. ''She says not. Maybe it's some unconscious thing. Take the others our love, will you?''

''On my way.''

Jeff turned his attention to Bailey and kissed her knuckles. ''All right, now let's see what we can do.'' He glanced at the monitor. ''Another contraction coming. You ready?''

''I'm ready.''

''I love you more than anything.''

''I know. I love you, too. What time is it?'' She tried to turn toward the clock, but he put a hand to the side of her face to prevent her and smiled into her eyes.

''Time to have this baby,'' he said. ''Please. For me?''

As the pain of the contraction overtook her, she looked past him to focus on the clock: 11:13. She smiled in the agony and ecstasy of transitional labor, formed a mental picture of her son, who would probably have blue eyes and a bossy disposition, and she hoped he'd hold out for another forty-seven minutes.

*Readers, don't miss
the heartwarming conclusion to
the* DELIVERY ROOM DADS *series:
BABY 2000 by Judy Christenberry
coming next month from
Harlequin American Romance!*

*This holiday season, dash to
the delivery room with*

HARLEQUIN®
AMERICAN ◆ ROMANCE®

Delivery
Room
DADS

**The McIntyre brothers of Bison City, Wyoming,
have no idea they're about to become daddies—
until a little stork tells them to hustle down to
the delivery room!**

*Don't miss this exciting new series from three of
your favorite American Romance® authors!*

October 1999
BABY BY MIDNIGHT?
by Karen Toller Whittenburg (#794)

November 1999
COUNTDOWN TO BABY
by Muriel Jensen (#798)

December 1999
BABY 2000
by Judy Christenberry (#802)

Available wherever Harlequin books are sold.

3 Stories of Holiday Romance from three bestselling Harlequin® authors

Valentine Babies

by
ANNE STUART

TARA TAYLOR QUINN

JULE MCBRIDE

Goddess in Waiting by Anne Stuart
Edward walks into Marika's funky maternity shop to pick up some things for his sister. He doesn't expect to assist in the delivery of a baby and fall for outrageous Marika.

Gabe's Special Delivery by Tara Taylor Quinn
On February 14, Gabe Stone finds a living, breathing valentine on his doorstep—his daughter. Her mother has given Gabe four hours to adjust to fatherhood, resolve custody and win back his ex-wife?

My Man Valentine by Jule McBride
Everyone knows Eloise Hunter and C. D. Valentine are in love. Except Eloise and C. D. Then, one of Eloise's baby-sitting clients leaves her with a baby to mind, and C. D. swings into protector mode.

VALENTINE BABIES

On sale January 2000 at your favorite retail outlet.

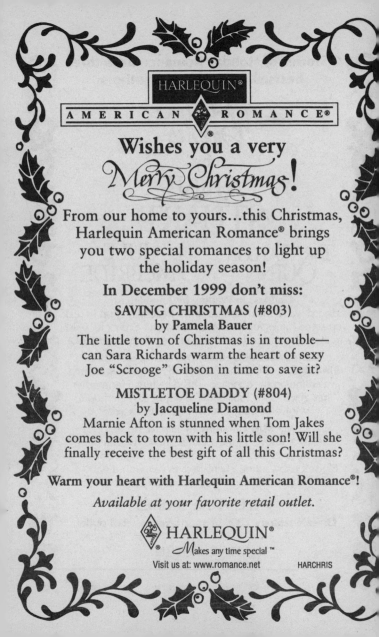